War Games

Sam had a problem.

He was supposed to be recuperating from a war disaster.

But three people were dead—and each time he had been the one to find the body.

Suddenly he was trapped in a bizarre game of unfaithful husbands, black revolution, espionage and murder.

How he yearned to get back to his nice, peaceful war . . .

Trouble Follows Me
A stunning suspense novel by
Ross Macdonald*

"Ross Macdonald gives to the detective story the accent of class that the late Raymond Chandler did."

—*Chicago Tribune*

*Originally published under the name of Kenneth Millar

TROUBLE FOLLOWS ME

Ross Macdonald

Originally published under the name of
KENNETH MILLAR

A NATIONAL GENERAL COMPANY

TROUBLE FOLLOWS ME

*A Bantam Book / published by arrangement with
the author*

PRINTING HISTORY
*Dodd, Mead edition published 1946 under the
name of Kenneth Millar*
Bantam edition published September 1972

*Bantam Books are published by Bantam Books, Inc., a National
General company. Its trade-mark, consisting of the words "Bantam
Books" and the portrayal of a bantam, is registered in the United
States Patent Office and in other countries. Marca Registrada.
Bantam Books, Inc., 666 Fifth Avenue, New York, N.Y. 10019.*

PRINTED IN THE UNITED STATES OF AMERICA

To
Donald Pearce

CONTENTS

PART I

OAHU

1

In February, 1945, Honolulu was a small blend of Los Angeles and prewar Shanghai, shaken up with the carnival end of a county fair, and poured out carelessly at the edge of the sea. Men in uniform, white, tan, khaki, grey, green, pullulated in the streets, looking for a place like home and not finding any.

We drove through town in Eric's jeep from the Pearl Harbor side, past miles of gift and curio shops, bars and lunchrooms, Turkish baths, photographers' studios, peepshows. Be Photographed with a Hula Girl. Dispenser General of Alcoholic Beverages. Real American Hot Dogs. Dance of the Seven Veils Only Five Cents.

I had seen it before and it hadn't changed, except that my year in the forward area made it seem more interesting and metropolitan. Still it was no substitute for Detroit.

"Where's the drink you promised me?" I said to Eric.

The traffic ahead of us had been temporarily jammed by a Navy Yard bus taking on a load of sailors. Eric was scowling over the wheel. He was a fair-haired man of thirty, with the leanness and boyish quick gestures of twenty, and almost all of its hair. Since I had last seen him his collar had sprouted the double silver bars of a full lieutenant. I had noticed when I first met him in the Administration Building that afternoon that his mouth and eyes were still undecided between cynicism and sensibility.

The bus finally moved, like the key log in a log-jam, and the stream of traffic flowed on with our jeep nosing into the middle of it.

"I said how about that drink you promised me."

"Hold your horses," Eric said. "What are you, a dipsomaniac or something?"

3

"I haven't had a drink since we left Guam. Before that I didn't have one for three months. Does that make me a dipsomaniac?"

"Apparently. Don't worry, there'll be plenty left for you."

"Doesn't the bar in Honolulu House close at six?"

"Theoretically it does. But we've all got bottles. If the drinking stopped at six, what would be the use of a ship's party?"

Honolulu House was a decaying mansion standing in its own grounds on the eastern outskirts of the city. A rich planter built it there between the mountains and the sea at the end of the nineteenth century, in the hope that his descendants would live there from generation to generation. When he died his sons and daughters moved back to the mainland, and the house degenerated by degrees into a club of uncertain membership.

It was a three-story frame structure with a wide verandah on four sides. When we arrived the garden of flowers which surrounded it was smouldering in a thin smoke of early twilight.

We parked the jeep at the rear and went into the basement bar. There was a blaze of light, noise and women. Two long tables ran half the length of the narrow brick-walled room to hold the whiskey bottles. We found two unoccupied chairs, and I took one while Eric started off to the bar for ice.

Before he got there he joined a group that was standing near the door. There was a small dark girl with curly black hair, a naval officer with a brown moustache and a Vandyke two shades lighter, a tall heavy man wearing a war correspondent's insignia, and a blonde with her profile to me, five feet seven inches of it. When I saw her the room came into focus and began to revolve about her like a shining wheel.

Eric had his head close to the dark girl's, and made no move to break away. I got up and joined the group, and Eric introduced me. The bearded man was Dr. Savo, surgeon of Eric's destroyer. The brunette with the keen pert face was Sue Sholto. The war correspondent was

4

Gene Halford. His thick jowls and the bald half of his head were darkened by a tan which only the tropics could have given him.

"You've heard of Mr. Halford," Eric said. "He writes for two magazines, and ninety-seven newspapers, isn't it, Gene?"

I hadn't heard of him, but I politely said I had.

"Sam used to be a newspaperman in Detroit himself."

"Is that a fact?" Halford said. I didn't like the faintly patronizing note in his voice, and I didn't like the fact that his left shoulder was behind the blonde girl's right shoulder, like a Reserved sign.

Her name was Mary Thompson. Their shoulders disengaged when she moved to give me her hand. When she smiled her eyes changed from blue to aquamarine. "I'm glad to meet you, Mr. Drake."

She was a tall blonde, but not the cornfed type. Her body was sleek and disciplined, so well made that she didn't look big. There was in her face a fascinating combination of things I liked and things I didn't understand. I wondered what I could do about it. A man like Halford with a million readers, even though he was forty and balding, had glamor. Gene Halford looked at her as if he knew it.

While I was groping for a gambit he ended the game. "Let's go out and get leis," he said to her. "There's an old woman selling them on the corner."

As they moved away, Mary Thompson gave me a smiling look which seemed to imply that she'd see me later. I got some ice at the bar and went back to the table where the bottles were. I made a little celibate ceremony out of mixing and drinking a double highball. I concentrated on the good sharp clean taste of the whiskey and soda, the feel of the ice against my teeth, the cold wet glass in the circle of my fingers. Then the small expanding glow in my stomach, spreading from there through my body like a blob of dye in a beaker of water, finally working into my brain, warming and coloring my perceptions.

5

The first stages of drunkenness are delicate, illusive and altruistic, like the first stages of love. I became very pleased with the bright disorderly room, the merry drunken laughter, the sweet chiding clink of ice in glasses, the confusion of shoptalk and woman-talk, war and love. What pleased me most was the fact that the room didn't move back and forth, sideways and diagonally. It was the most lovably stable room I had sat in for a long time.

"How you doing, Sam?" Eric sat down beside me and poured himself a drink.

"I was just thinking that I like this room and everybody in it. Even the lieutenant commanders. Where's your girl-friend?"

"Went up to the powder-room to do her hair. But she's not my girl-friend."

"I'm not likely to tell Helen about it. That girl likes you pretty well."

"I know it," he said. His mood, which was evident in his face, was an uncomfortable mixture of vanity and shame. Vanity because he had a pretty girl in love with him. Shame because he had a wife in Michigan and should know better. "If you ever did tell Helen, it'd be just too bad."

"Why should I?"

"Anyway, there's nothing to tell." He shrugged his shoulders awkwardly, and his fair transparent skin showed a flush. "It seems funny that you'll be seeing Helen in a week or two. I haven't seen her for two years."

"I'll look her up when I get home. Anything special you want me to tell her?"

"Hell, tell her I'm healthy. And, of course, I love her. Tell her there's no danger when we're operating around Pearl like this. She never believes me when I write her that in letters."

He finished his drink, very quickly I thought. I poured him another and filled my own glass.

"They're at it again," Eric said. "Always talking about the war."

An ensign with wings, across the table from us, was telling a faded blonde how it felt to go in through ack-ack at five hundred feet. He said it didn't feel so bad because you didn't really believe it until afterwards. Now the real hell was night landings on a jeep carrier. . . .

"It's on everybody's mind," I said.

"But we're not supposed to talk about it." He had once had a one-week course in Washington on security, and it left its mark on him. "Past operations aren't so bad, but when they talk about the big operation that's coming up—"

"Now you're doing it."

"The hell I am." But he colored. "If I was an enemy spy right here this afternoon—"

"You wouldn't have been born in Toledo and you'd have funny little slant eyes and people would point the finger of scorn at you."

"Don't kid yourself. The Japs are willing to spend money, and there are Caucasians who like money better than anything else."

"Say you were a spy and managed to crash an officers' party and picked up some information. You could gloat over it in private, but I don't see what else you could do with it. The leaks have been plugged since December 7 a long time ago."

Sue Sholto appeared at the foot of the stairs and came across the room toward us. The movements of her small perfect body were birdlike and precise. I had the impression that she came back to Eric like a hawk to a wrist. We stood up and she sat down between Eric and me. He poured her a drink, and another for himself. Her brilliant dark eyes followed the movements of his hands, but he didn't seem to notice.

He sipped his drink and said: "Maybe they have been plugged. But I'll bet a smart operative could find a way."

"What on earth are you talking about, Eric? You look silly when you get so solemn."

"Sam doesn't think there's any way an enemy agent could get information out of these islands. What do you think? You work in a radio station."

"That's a funny question to ask a girl. I never thought

7

of it. In spy stories they always have a secret transmitter hidden in the mountains, don't they?"

"That's out," I said. "With the direction-finders we've got now, we'd put the finger on an illegal transmitter two hours after it opened up. The nearest Jap islands are a long way from here now. It takes a lot of power to reach them."

"You wouldn't have to reach the nearest Jap island," Eric said. "There are Jap subs in these waters. They can surface at night. They could pick up a weak broadcast and relay it to Tokyo."

"But we'd hear both broadcasts," I said. "And naturally we'd put a stop to them. There are plenty of Japs here, and no doubt some of them are secretly loyal to the old country. But I still don't see what they can do about it."

"Do about what?" a hard deep voice said behind me. It was Gene Halford. He and Mary Thompson had come back, wearing yellow leis.

Eric and I stood up and they sat down with us, Mary between me and Halford. Her yellow garland made her eyes as bright blue as cornflowers. Her hair was fragrant and shining, like pull-taffy. Her linen suit had a clean smell.

Sue Sholto's dark eyes were turned inward, looking at something behind drawn blinds in her mind. "We were talking about how the enemy could get secret information out of the islands." She spoke as if with an effort.

"I suppose you could send a letter to a neutral country," Mary said. "Using a code of course. You know, 'Uncle Harry has a cold' means 'The Americans have a new battleship at Pearl Harbor.' "

"That's pretty old hat," I said. "Don't forget we've got a pretty efficient censorship."

Eric spoke meditatively. "I wonder if a small boat could get out to a Jap sub."

"Not a chance," I said. "You know the restrictions on boating around here better than I do."

Halford's muddy green eyes had been watching us alertly. Now he spread his thick hands on the table with a slapping sound that made my nerves wince. He had the air of a man who habitually took possession of situations, then bestowed them on the original owners as his personal gift.

"Aren't we being just a little indiscreet?" he said heavily. "Inasmuch as there is a leak of information from Pearl Harbor?"

"There is?" I repeated idiotically.

"You're in the Navy, men. I thought you knew. Public Relations and Censorship keep pounding into us correspondents that civilians mustn't be allowed to know what the Navy knows. I never thought it might be the other way around."

"Where did you get this information?" I asked.

"I have my sources. I know a good many things that I can't print. For God's sake keep your lips buttoned over that one."

"My lips are well-buttoned. There's a gap in yours where the wind blows through."

A dark flush, darker in contrast with the clear yellow of his lei, mounted from his neck through his jowls, to his padded cheekbones. I wondered if I was going to have an opportunity to hit him. A year in the forward area sharpens your combative instincts and makes you want to hit people you don't like.

But all he said was: "The original indiscretion was not mine, I believe."

"Indiscretion, hell," Eric said. "We were talking hypothetically."

"Couldn't we just go on talking hypothetically?" Sue said in a little-girl tone. "There wasn't so much electricity in the air when it was hypothetical."

"Let's put it down as scuttlebutt," I said. "It's perfectly possible that Mr. Halford doesn't know what he's talking about."

Halford gave me a malevolent look. But if he argued he'd have to insist that he had made a bad break. He didn't argue.

"It's getting terribly close in here," Mary said brightly. "They're serving supper at the buffet upstairs by now. I'm starved."

9

We decided to have supper. I picked up one of our bottles, which was two parts empty, and brought it along. The manager, rigid in his dusty tuxedo like a guard in uniform, was standing at the head of the stairs. There was a smile of strained affability on his sallow Eurasian face.

"Please don't handle the bottle quite so conspicuously, sir," he said to me. "It's after six, and we don't want any trouble."

"O.K., we'll foil the revenooers."

"I'll take it," Mary said. She put the bottle in her big straw handbag. Sue took Eric's.

We found an empty table on the verandah on the side away from the street. The sea was barely visible from there. While I watched it night took a giant step down from the mountains and sucked up the last grey light from its surface.

The blonde girl was standing beside me.

I said abruptly: "Are you with Halford? If you are I'll fade out."

"I'm not. I barely know him." She touched my arm lightly with her fingers. "Don't fade out."

Halford and Eric had gone to join the line at the buffet, and I followed them. Before Halford got there Mrs. Merriwell intercepted him and did me a service. Mrs. Merriwell was a lady of uncertain age, but not so very uncertain. Her hair was arranged in stiffly curled bangs which masked the wrinkles on her forehead. Nothing could mask the two harsh lines which drooped from her bleak nose to her brilliantly painted mouth. Her brown eyes were restless and shrill. The natural shrillness of her voice was softened by a South Carolina accent.

"Why, Gene Halford," she said in pleased surprise. "I've been looking for you all afternoon."

She looked expectantly at Eric and me, and Halford introduced us. Mrs. Merriwell was delighted, she was sure, and it certainly was a very authentic thrill for her to meet us-all. We-all lined up at the buffet where the wardroom stewards of Eric's destroyer were serving supper. Mrs. Merriwell thought she would have a teensy bit of chicken salad, and perhaps a mite of a sandwich.

10

There was a look of stultified protest on Halford's face, but he wasn't drunk enough to shake her off. The four of us went back to the table on the verandah together. I carried Mary's plate and sat beside her. We had a round of drinks which Eric poured under the table.

"Here's to the old Dog-Dog," Eric said. "How do you think the party's going?"

For him, the party seemed to be going well. His light blue eyes glittered damply. He was turned towards Sue Sholto so that their knees must have been touching under the table.

"I like it fine," I said, and looked at Mary.

Halford produced an appreciative grin from some reserve that Mrs. Merriwell had not yet touched.

"I think it's lovely, simply lovely," said Mrs. Merriwell. "All you handsome young men in your uniforms. The stewards in their white coats. You know, it reminds me of our old club, in the days before my dear deceased husband— But I mustn't talk of that: I mustn't even think of it."

She lowered her eyes, saw her highball, and took a long swallow.

"It is a bit like the old South, isn't it?" Eric leaned forward slightly, his face serious. "I often wonder whether it's a good thing."

"Whether what's a good thing?" Sue said in her child's voice. "What's a good thing?"

"I have my doubts about our policy of concentrating Negroes in the menial jobs. This quarter I happen to be treasurer of our wardroom mess, and it's partly my responsibility to supervise the stewards. I often think their morale would be higher, and they'd be more useful into the bargain, if they didn't feel so darn limited."

"I agree with you," Mrs. Merriwell cried. "I thoroughly agree with you. Everyone should be given an equal chance, even niggers. Naturally they'll never reach the position in life of a white man. But I say, give all an equal opportunity, unless, of course, they show they don't deserve it."

"How could a black man deserve the same things as an

11

Anglo-Saxon?" Sue said quietly. There was a hostile and sardonic glitter in her dark eyes, but Mrs. Merriwell didn't notice it.

"You know, sometimes I feel inclined to agree with you. There's something so unpleasant about a black skin. And the way that big buck looked at me when he was serving my salad—It really gave me the shivers."

"Hector Land?" Eric said. "The big bruiser with the broken nose?"

"Yes, that's the one. Those radicals in Washington talk about social equality, and that's all well and good, but I couldn't bear to sit down at the same table with a nigger. I'd feel contaminated."

"But you don't mind eating food that they've prepared," Sue said. "In fact you greatly enjoy the idea."

"I don't know what you mean."

"I'm Jewish," Sue said. Her eyes were burning black. Her voice was hard. She was quite drunk. "So I have some faint idea of what it feels like to be a Negro. Other things being equal, I prefer Negroes to whites. Especially unreconstructed Southern whites."

"Well!" said Mrs. Merriwell. The word made a rushing sound in her mouth. She stood up with her unfinished plate in one hand and her highball in the other. "You said you wanted to talk to me privately, Gene. Are you coming?"

Halford got up unwillingly, murmured his excuse, and went into the house at her angry clicking heels.

"That's an insult she'll never get over," I said to Mary. "Who is she?"

"Secretary to one of the men at Hickam. She's probably one of Halford's sources."

Eric's angular face was very stiff, on the point of crumpling in anger or despair. "You shouldn't talk like that," he said to Sue. "She'll tell everybody in town that you're a nigger-lover."

"I don't give a damn," she said in a high thin voice. "Maybe I am."

His face reddened and grew pale in blotches. "Excuse me. How interesting."

12

"And don't try to snub me, either, my ambulating ego. Have you always confined yourself strictly to Mem Sahibs? Pray tell us about your amorous exploits, gentlemen."

She was so evidently drunk that Eric decided he needn't take her seriously. "You're getting as tight as a tick, my girl. No more liquor for you. Can't anyone, for God's sake, think of an impersonal subject to talk about?"

"We were talking about love," I said. "There's nothing more impersonal than love. Everybody has it, shows the same symptoms, and does the same things about them."

"Nonsense," Mary said pleasantly. "Love is a highly individual art. A great many people aren't even capable of it. From what you just said, I suspect you're one of them."

"From what you just said, I suspect you aren't."

An orchestra began to play in the ballroom. Sue told Eric that she would like to dance. They went away together in unconscious step, as if they knew each other very well and lived by the same fundamental rhythms. She was clinging a little blindly to his arm. As they passed through the door into the bright light, he looked down at her with anxious tenderness in the very set of his shoulders.

"Sue and Eric are old friends, aren't they?" I said.

"For a year or so, I guess. He looks her up whenever he's in port. She's in love with him."

"It's funny he didn't mention her to me before we got here."

"No it isn't. The affair isn't going too well. Eric's married, isn't he?"

"Yes, I know his wife. She's crazy about him. I think he's gotten himself into a box."

"Sue's the one to be sorry for." Her glance passed over my face swiftly. "Are you married?"

"No. It'd be quite safe to dance with me, I think."

It was a six-piece scratch orchestra, but she danced so well that she made me feel expert and daring. Her high heels made her almost as tall as I was, and I had a chance to study her face. It was a Leonardo face, with full red

13

lips, a straight and passionate nose, high delicate temples, and mutable eyes that altered with her mood in color, depth, and meaning. Her body was whalebone and plush. Her legs were a perfect rhyme.

After a couple of dances she said, "I have to go pretty soon."

"Why?"

"I go on the air at nine-fifteen."

"Say, you're not the girl that announces the record programs?"

"Sue and I alternate. Have you heard us?"

"The last few nights I have, when we were coming in. No wonder I felt as if I'd known you before."

"Don't be irrelevant. I want to know what you think of the programs."

"I liked them. I like your voice, too. It's funny I didn't recognize it."

"It's always different over the air."

The music started again and we danced to it. I couldn't see Sue and Eric on the floor.

"Any criticisms?" Mary said.

"No. Well, not enough Ellington. There's never enough Ellington on any record program. Too much *Don't Fence Me In.* I admire both Crosby and Cole Porter, but I can imagine a more fortunate marriage of their talents."

"I know, but a lot of people like it. And the best Ellington aren't so easy to get. I broke our *Portrait of Bert Williams* last week, and I almost sat right down and cried."

"Pinch me somebody quick. The girl in the dream always liked *Portrait of Bert Williams.*"

"You wouldn't like it if I pinched you. I'm a very intense pincher. What dream?"

"The dream I had. I'm a very intense dreamer. And it worked. The dream came real."

She pulled back a little and looked levelly into my eyes. "You say it well. Have you been out a long time?"

"Just a year. It seemed like a long time. That's why the dream was necessary."

"Don't make me feel like a necessity. Since I came out

14

here I've learned how it feels to be something there's a shortage of."

"The last pack of cigarettes under the counter?"

"The scrap of meat thrown to the wolves. I'd rather feel like a human being."

"There's barely a trace of canine in my nature."

She withdrew her eyes, and because I wanted them back I changed my tack:

"How long have you been out here?"

"Just a few months. Five and a half."

"Are you from Ohio, Michigan, or Illinois?"

"Your ear's pretty good. I lived in Cleveland. What time is it?"

"Eight-thirty."

"I'll have to leave at the end of this dance."

"Let me drive you over. I can borrow Eric's jeep."

"That would be nice. I haven't seen Eric or Sue for quite a while, though. Maybe they're out in the garden."

While Mary went upstairs to get her coat, I searched the first floor for Eric and Sue. They weren't on the dance-floor, they weren't in the darkened dining-room, though other couples were. I walked clear around the house on the verandah, but I couldn't find them. The night was very dark. There was a full moon, but almost opaque clouds showed where it was only by a faint glow. Cascades of lights were twinkling far up the hills, but the dark clouds which squatted heavily and eternally on Oahu's peaks loomed against the sky like a dismal fate.

I decided against searching the garden, because it would be embarrassing. There were soft voices among the flowers, and shadowy double shapes both vertical and horizontal.

When I found Eric eventually, he was by himself. He was sitting on an upturned wastebasket in a corner of the men's head, nursing a dying bottle of bourbon. The damp glitter in his eyes had frozen into glassiness. His thin lips were loose and purplish. His torso was lax and wavering. There were individual drops of sweat oozing from his hairline onto his blank forehead. Once or twice I had seen men drunker, but they were not able to sit up.

"Sue's gone away and left me," he said in a muffled singsong. "She went away and left me all alone. She's a hellish woman, Sam. Don't ever get mixed up with those little dark babies. They're deadly nightshade. You can't get over 'em."

I wasn't enjoying the conversation, and didn't want to keep Mary waiting. "Will you lend me your jeep? I should be back in an hour."

He found the key after a laborious exploration of his clothes. "Take it away, Sam. I don't know where you're going and I don't care."

"You'd better go upstairs and lie down."

"Don't want to lie down. Sit here until the cows come home. Here with the writing on the wall. Lovely writing on the wall, expresses my sentiments." He chanted several four-letter words. "There's my sentiments. Bloody but unbowed. A jug of wine and thou beside me singing in the urinal." He giggled.

I went away from his unhappy nonsense and got to the lobby in time to be waiting when Mary came downstairs. She looked a little pale and tense.

"Is Sue up there?"

"No. I thought she might be lying down in the powder-room. She drank too much before supper. But there's nobody there."

"She probably went home. Eric's in bad condition. I found him in the john."

"Perhaps she did. I'll call from the studio."

It was a five-minute drive to the broadcasting station. When we got there Mary left me on a folding chair in the darkened audience room, and went to phone. She came back in a minute and said in a worried voice:

"She isn't at home, at least not yet. I hope she didn't pass out somewhere."

"She'll turn up," I said.

"I still have a few minutes before the broadcast. Would you like to look at the record library? Or would you rather stay and listen to them?"

She moved her head towards the glassed-in broadcast-ing room. Five or six Hawaiians wearing rather dirty leis were playing ukuleles, steel guitars, and a bull fiddle. The current tune was *Blue Hawaii*.

I said: "I think I can tear myself away from all this exotic glamor."

She led me down a dark passageway to a door which she unlocked. She found the switch and turned on the lights in the record library. It was a high-ceilinged narrow room completely lined with shelves which were filled with records. She showed me the various sections: the classics, the semi-classics, the new popular hits, the stand-bys which never grow old, the transcribed programs from the big American chains, and a set of big discs on which complete Armed Services programs were recorded.

I saw a record I knew, took it off the shelf and handed it to her. "Play this."

She put the record on a turntable. It was Fats Waller's *Ain't Misbehavin'*, the organ version. We stood together and listened to the lilting melancholy music which Waller had squeezed out of an organ in Paris years ago. I half-turned toward her, impelled by the powerful sexuality of the music. Perhaps she recognized my intention. She said in a brisk technical way:

"Any questions?"

When the record was finished, I said: "I did a little broadcasting when I was in college. They used to be pretty strict about timing our scripts. How do you time record programs?"

"It's easy enough with the one-disc programs. They're already timed when we get them. And some of the ninety-sixes and hundred-and-twelves are standardized."

"Ninety-sixes?"

"Ninety-six turns to a record. They go around ninety-six times. The ones that are specially made for broadcasting are standardized so that you can measure the time right on the record. They send us a little ruler with them, laid out in units of time instead of inches."

"That means that the speed of the turntable must be standardized too."

"That's right. But the ordinary platters which Sue and I mostly use aren't standardized. The grooving may even

17

vary from one side to the other, depending on the kind of music."

"I don't get it."

"Whether the music is high or low. It'd take too long to explain. You can always time a record by playing it ahead of time, of course. But often we just trust to luck. If we have to fill in at the end we can always let the theme-song run through twice instead of once. It isn't as if we were on a national hookup."

She glanced at an electric clock in a corner of the room. It was ten minutes after nine. "I've got to leave you now."

"Can I help you carry the records, or anything?"

"Oh, no thanks. They're already in by the mike. We've got a boy, a little Chinese, who takes them in in a cart."

She turned out the lights, locked the door, and left me at the entrance to the soundproof room. I listened to the broadcast through the loudspeaker in the audience room. Her voice was deep for a woman, and steady, the only kind of female speaking voice that sounds well over the air. She went in for quietly kidding her audience, more by inflecting her voice than by what she said.

I gathered that she had fan-mail. Most of the records she played were requests. I began to compose a fan-letter to her in my head. Though her low voice flooded the room when she spoke, vibrating in every corner, she seemed very remote behind the plate-glass partition. Very remote and desirable. Before I had put into the letter all the things I wanted to say, the broadcast was over.

"All set to go back?" I said when she rejoined me. "It's only half an hour till curfew."

"I have a curfew pass, on account of the midnight broadcasts. I don't want to go home till I make sure Sue is all right."

"She'll be all right. I may have to carry Eric up the gangplank, though."

When we got back to Honolulu House the party was at its climax. One of the officers had joined the orchestra and was tearing off hot licks on a clarinet as high as a kite. A fat jiggling woman was dancing in the middle of the floor, snapping her fingers and letting out periodic squeals. A

18

weaving ring of men and women, which included Halford and Mrs. Merriwell, was dancing around and around her. Two or three indefatigable couples were jitterbugging at their own end of the room, leaping and whirling in mad silent ecstasy. Other couples were leaving.

We found Eric lying stone cold, but snoring passionately, on a settee in the dining-room. The big Negro steward whom he had called Hector Land was hovering over him as if he thought something should be done but didn't know what.

"Just leave him for now," I said. "If he doesn't come out of it in the next few minutes I'll take him back to the ship."

"Yessir. I just wanted to ask him if we could get any more ice. We're all out of ice."

"It doesn't make any difference now, anyway. Have you seen Miss Sholto? The young lady who was with Mr. Swann at supper?"

"No, sir. I haven't seen her all night. Maybe she's out in the garden."

"Shall we try the garden?" Mary said.

We went out the back door and stood on the verandah for a minute, letting our eyes get used to the darkness. I put my hand on her waist but she turned away out of my grasp.

"Don't be premature," she said seriously. "I came to this party to drink and dance, not to be made love to."

"Premature is a good word. There's a future in it."

"Is there? You talk ahead of yourself. I like the way you talk, though."

"Words used to be my business."

"That's the trouble. I don't know whether there's much connection between what you say and what you are. A lot of servicemen away from home have lost track of themselves. God, am I talking like a Sunday School teacher?"

"Go right ahead. A woman's softening influence is just what I need."

"It's true of all of us, I guess. Not just servicemen.

19

There aren't many people I know that haven't lost track of themselves."

It was queer to be talked at that way by a blonde I was trying to make, but what she said struck home. Ever since I left Detroit I had felt dislocated, and after my ship went down it was worse. Sometimes I felt that all of us were adrift on a starless night, singing in the dark, full of fears and laughing them off with laughter which didn't fool anyone.

On this side of the house the verandah was roofless. I looked up at the night sky hanging huge over the mountains. The somber clouds on the peaks parted for a moment and let the moon sail through, trailing a single bright star like a target sleeve.

"I think that's what must have happened to Eric and Sue," I said. "They thought it didn't matter, and it turned into very bad medicine for both of them."

"I wonder if she'll ever be happy again," Mary said.

I wasn't listening. Something against the wall of the house had caught my eye, and I looked up and found Sue Sholto in the moonlight. Her head was cocked birdlike on one side as if she was waiting for the answer to a question, and her tongue protruded roguishly. Under her dangling feet were three yards of empty air. Her whole slight weight was supported by a yellow rope knotted under her ear. Her eyes were larger and blacker than they had been in life.

2

THE clouds came together again, blotting out the moon, like shadowy giants huddled in a conference of evil. But not before Mary had followed my look and seen what I saw.

"She's killed herself," she said in a high unnatural voice. "I was afraid something had happened to her." She beat her clenched fists together with a dull futile sound. "I should have stayed with her."

"Do you know what room that is? Nobody could reach her from here." I gestured upward and my hand flew higher than I intended, out of my control. We looked up again. With the moon gone Sue Sholto was an obscure shadow hanging over us. Only her feet were visible in the light from below, stirring almost imperceptibly with the twist in the hemp. There was a hole in the toe of one of her stockings, and I could see the red polish shining on a toenail.

"I think it's the ladies' room, but I can't be sure. It looks out the back."

"Stay downstairs with the people," I said. "I'll go up."

I found Lieutenant Savo, the ship's doctor, on the dance floor. When I told him what I had seen his Vandyke wobbled once and set firmly. He was up the stairs ahead of me.

The ladies' room was actually three rooms with interconnecting doors: a well-lighted dressing-room with mirrors and a dressing table, a washroom on one side of it, and on the other a dark little room containing nothing more than a few armchairs and a couch. Dr. Savo had attended a girl at a previous party in this room, and he explained that it was used only in case of sickness or alcoholic coma.

I found the light switch and saw that the room had been used for something else. The couch, wide, lumpy and chintz-covered, was jammed against the wall under the sill of the single window. Tied around its bowed walnut legs was the other end of the yellow rope which supported Sue Sholto. We drew her up through the open window and found that she was easy to lift. But in the harsh light cast by the obsolete ceiling chandelier she was not easy to look at. The noose under her ear was clumsily knotted but it had served its purpose. There was nothing left in her face which Eric Swann could have loved.

I went into the next room to get a towel to hide it. Mary was standing in the hall doorway, very pale and tall.

"She's dead, isn't she?"

"Yes. Don't come in."

There were footsteps in the hall, and Eric appeared at her shoulder. His flesh was the color of a dead man's and his eyes were set as if he had forgotten to blink them.

"Something's happened to Sue," he said.

Mary moved out of his way and he pushed me aside without knowing it. It would have been a thankless job to fight him for the sake of saving him nightmares. He said to the dead woman: "Darling, you shouldn't have done it. I'd have done anything."

Then he lay down on the floor beside her and hid his face in her hair, which flourished on the dusty rug like a black forest. A man's dry crying is a poor imitation of a woman's melodious weeping, but it is more terrible in its effect. His retching sobs opened another trapdoor in the bottom cellar of pity and horror. I shut the door on him so Mary wouldn't see.

"Where did she get the rope?" I asked.

"There's one in every upstairs room. Look." She pointed to a hook beside the dressing-room windows where another yellow rope hung in a coil. I had an instinctive desire to take it away and burn it.

"What in God's name do they leave things like that around for?"

"It's a fire escape, the only one they have."

"And I suppose they serve you hemlock with your

dinner, just in case you want to take a sip or two between courses in the Socratic manner."

"Don't talk so much and for God's sake don't try to be funny," Mary said wearily. "You hardly knew Sue, but I did." Her neck drooped like a wilting flower's stalk, and there was nothing I could do for her at all.

A petty officer wearing a black and yellow Shore Patrol armband came into the room with four or five people at his heels. Their faces were blankly eager. I thought of a pack of necrophagous jackals. Mrs. Merriwell was one of them, and the Eurasian manager, tense and stammering, was another.

The SP man, who was young and worried-looking, said: "My name's Baker, sir. I understand there's been a very bad accident."

"Come into the next room. The value of publicity is sometimes over-estimated—"

"Accident nothing," Mrs. Merriwell bayed. "I don't believe it was suicide. That awful nigger was up in that very room. I saw him in the hallway coming out."

"When was this?" Baker said. "And who are you talking about, Madam?"

"That horrible black steward, the one with the crumpled ears. He'd have frightened me out of my wits up here if I didn't know how to handle niggers. I believe he raped that girl and hanged her to cover up."

Baker looked at me and then at the door to the inner room. I nodded, and he opened the door wide enough to slip through. The door opened again a moment later and Eric came out awkwardly as if propelled from behind. He looked at the little crowd in the doorway like an amateur actor facing his first audience. I told them that if they had to wait it would have to be in the hall. Mary got up and moved out with them.

"What right have you, young man?" said Mrs. Merriwell. I shut the door in her face.

Eric sat down in front of the dressing table on a stool covered with cheap yellow lace. He examined his face in the mirror with profound intensity, as if he was seeing it for the first time. Grief has curious gestures, and this was

23

one of them. His face didn't please him, and he turned away.

"I don't look so good," he said tonelessly.

"No."

"Why do you suppose she did it, Sam?"

"I don't know, I hardly knew her."

"Could she have killed herself because she loved me? I mean because I couldn't marry her?"

"She could have. But if that's true don't ever let yourself be proud of it."

"You're pretty brass-tacks tonight," Eric said, with a thin wire of self-pity running through his tone.

"I found her. If you helped to put her where I found her, I've got a grudge against you. If you didn't, I'm sorry for you. I'm sorry for you anyway."

"I'll be all right tomorrow," he said. But he said it as if he knew that certain kinds of pictures fade slowly even in sunlight.

Dr. Savo came out of the inner room with Baker, the petty officer, who looked a year or two older.

"There's no sign of assault," the doctor said. "There are a couple of bruises on her back, but she must have got them climbing out of the window, or swinging against the wall when she dropped. It's funny nobody saw her or heard her. They usually go into pretty violent convulsions."

"Thank you, sir," Baker said. "I'll have to call the civilian police, and I guess they'll be holding an inquest on the body. I never had anything like this come up before. I've seen a couple of guys knocked out, but—"

"Forget it if you can," Savo said. "That's one thing I learned in medical school."

There was a loud bickering noise in the hall, of several voices raised in argument. I opened the door and saw the Negro, Land, standing in the hallway surrounded by Mrs. Merriwell and her little group. He was directly under a ceiling light, and I had my first good look at him.

His ears were convoluted and frayed like black rosebuds after a hailstorm. His nose was broad and saddled, his eyes bright black slits between pads of dead tissue. It was an old boxer's head, powerful and scarred as if it had once been used as a battering ram, set forward on a columnar neck as if it was ready to be used again. But there was no power in the posture of his body. His shoulders drooped forward and his belly heaved with his breathing. His wide hands were half-curled and turned to the light, which shone on the polished dark-pink palms. He looked like a frightened bear caught in a dog-pack.

"I didn't have anything to do with it," he was saying. "I didn't even know she was up here. I swear to God I didn't."

"What were you doing up here?" said an aging lieutenant whose face drooped like a hound's.

"I wasn't up here, boss—sir. I never set eyes on the young lady."

"I saw you," Mrs. Merriwell said, apparently not for the first time. "I saw you coming out of that door. He killed her," she said to the others, "I know he did. You can see that he's guilty just to look at him."

Land glanced at the ceiling, the whites of his eyes glaring.

His eyes shifted right and left, and stopped on me and Eric Swann standing in the doorway. His white steward's coat was turning dark with sweat. He must have given himself up for lost, for he said to Eric:

"I was up here, Mr. Swann, I admit that—"

"You see?" said Mrs. Merriwell. "He admits it." She looked at Eric triumphantly as if to say: You needed a lesson in race relations, my little man, and now, by God, you're getting it. "Officer," she said to Baker, "I demand that you arrest this man."

"What were you doing up here?" Eric said.

"I was looking for a drink. I know I did wrong, but that's all I was doing, looking for a drink."

"I don't understand."

"I was looking for somebody's bottle to take a drink out of. Sometimes some of the young ladies leave their bottles up here, and that's what I was looking for. I didn't find any, and then I heard somebody coming. I didn't see Miss Sholto at all."

25

"Come in here, Land," Dr. Savo said from the room behind me. "I can settle one point anyway. I'll ask the rest of you to leave the room, eh?"

"I wouldn't stay alone with him, sir," the manager said. "We wouldn't want anything else to happen."

"You wouldn't, eh?" Savo said as he shut the door of the dressing-room.

Mary was standing behind Mrs. Merriwell, looking tired and wan. I moved to her side.

"That's a ridiculous story," Mrs. Merriwell was saying. "Looking for a bottle!"

"Sue had a bottle in there," Mary said, and bit her lip as if she regretted saying it. More carrion for the jackals, I thought.

"Perhaps she did," Mrs. Merriwell said. "Perhaps she invited the boy in there with her. You never can tell what a nigger-lover will do."

Nor what Mrs. Merriwell will say, I thought. Eric looked at her with something like incredulity, but said nothing. Mary took hold of my arm, her fingers clenching painfully, and leaned her weight on me. For the first time in my life I began to see clearly what Dante saw, that hell is largely composed of conversations.

Dr. Savo opened the door and said briskly to Mrs. Merriwell: "What you suggest is out of the question. Shall I give you the physiological details?"

"Certainly not," said Mrs. Merriwell. She lifted her nose and tremulously sniffed the air. "But I think some disciplinary action is called for. At best, he came up here to steal."

"He'll be taken care of," Eric said. "Don't worry."

Mary's grip on my arm had relaxed, but she said: "I'm very tired. Do you think I can get home now?"

"I imagine we'll have to wait for the civilian police. After all, we were the ones."

"That found her, you mean?"

"It's after curfew, anyway. Before we can get back to Pearl we'll have to get a pass."

"You'll be able to get it through the police."

"It's queer they haven't come yet."

26

I looked around for Baker but he had disappeared. Nearly everyone had left the second floor. But Hector Land was still in the dressing-room when I looked in. He was sitting incongruously on the little yellow stool with his knees spread and his arms hanging straight down between them. In his face only his eyes seemed alive, but they were bright and moving.

Eric was standing in front of the door to the inner room, staring at Land without seeing him. He was staring harder with eyes at the back of his head which could look through doors. Dr. Savo was watching him.

"You should go back to the ship and get some sleep," he said to Eric. "You took an awful beating from the bottle before this happened." Eric didn't seem to hear him.

"What happened to Baker?" I said. "Did he go to call the police?"

"Right. They should be here now."

Mary sat down in an armchair by the window, and I leaned on the arm between her and the coiled rope. She let her head rest against the back of the chair, and her full white throat looked very vulnerable. Nothing was said for what seemed a long time. Perhaps it was only four or five minutes, but the minutes had to chisel their way through stone.

Finally I heard the irregular rhythm of several pairs of feet on the stairs and in the hall. Baker came into the room with a native police sergeant in olive drab, and a man in grey civilian clothes and a panama hat. He introduced the civilian as Detective Cram.

Cram took off his hat quickly and jerkily. He was a thin middle-sized, middle-aged man with a hair-trigger smile and frown. They alternated on his face but scarcely changed his expression of cynical curiosity. His mouth was thin, wide and knowing like a shark's. In a blue polka-dotted bow-tie and a striped silk shirt he looked a little too dapper to be quite real.

"O.K.," he said. "There's been an accident. Show it to me."

Savo took him into the inner room. When he came out there was no change in his face or voice.

"You were the one that found it, eh?" He pointed an eye at me. I said yes.

"Tell me about it." I told him about it.

"So the young lady was with you on the back porch. O.K., I won't ask what you were doing there."

"We were looking for Sue," Mary said stiffly.

"Friend of yours?"

"Yes. We worked in the same place."

"You worked at the station with her, eh? Any suggestions as to why she committed suicide?"

"I didn't know her that well. She didn't say anything to me."

"Maybe she wouldn't have to say anything to you?"

"I don't know," Mary said.

"Who was with her?" He jerked a thumb towards the door behind him. His eyes picked out Eric. "You?"

"Yes."

"Quarrel?"

"Yes."

"How long had you known her?"

"A year, I guess."

"Pretty well, eh?"

Eric's grief had carried him beyond reticence. For the time being he was shocked into candor, almost a childish naïveté. "We were in love with each other," he said.

"For Christ's sake, then," Cram said tonelessly, "why didn't you get married? She's no good to anybody now."

"I am married."

"I see. Congratulations. And the next thing you'll ask me is can't I hush this whole god-damn mess up for you."

"I haven't asked you anything," Eric said. "But now I'll ask you to go to hell."

"Sure sure. Cooperation is all I get. Who's this?" He looked at Land, who was still sitting by himself watching the rest of the room as if he expected it to close in on him suddenly without warning.

"Hector Land, sir. I'm a steward on Mr. Swann's ship."

"You own it, eh?" Cram said to Eric. "What's he here for?"

"He came here to serve at the party."

"Some woman accused him of murdering the girl," Savo put in. "Raping her and murdering her. He didn't."

"How do you know?"

"I'm a doctor."

"And I'm a cop, but I don't know a god-damn thing. How do you know?"

"I examined both of them." Savo glanced at Mary.

"I get it. Are those her shoes in there?"

"I could tell you," Mary said.

"Go and get them," Cram said to the sergeant. "They're at the end of the couch under the window."

They were black pumps, about size 4. Mary looked at them and said they were Sue's.

"They were off when you found her, eh?"

"Yes," I said. "She was in her stocking feet."

"I guess she took them off to climb out of the window," Cram said. "Well, I'll see you all at the inquest."

"When will that be?" I said.

"Tomorrow, if I can light a fire under a couple of comics downtown. Why?"

"I'm awaiting transportation to the mainland. I may get it tomorrow. Is there any chance of my signing a statement if the inquest isn't held in time?"

"Can't wait, eh? How the hell do I know? Everybody pushes me around. Craziest thing I ever did in my life was take off my army uniform."

"You were in the army, eh?" I said. "Is that why you don't like the navy?"

"I don't like the army either. I was in the last war. *You* know, the easy war."

"What you need is sleep, Inspector. Why don't you go home and take it?"

"Can't sleep. You're a doctor," he said to Savo. "What should I do if I can't sleep?"

"Drink whiskey," Savo said. "You wouldn't be so nervous if you got drunk every few days."

"I can't get drunk, either. On the jump all the goddamn time. Anyway, at twenty-five dollars a bottle what would I be doing with whiskey on my salary?"

"Would you mind jumping somewhere and getting us curfew passes?" I said. "Or have you got one in your marsupial pouch?"

"A kangaroo, get it, sergeant?" Cram said.

"No, sir."

"Let it pass. I can drive you out to the Navy Yard, I guess. After that you're on your own."

"What about Miss Thompson?"

"Live in town?"

"Yes," Mary said. "Quite near here."

"We'll drop you." He said to the sergeant, "You stay here. They'll probably come for her soon."

When we went downstairs there was nothing left of the party but overflowing ashtrays, empty and half-empty glasses which hung a sour smell in the air, chairs grouped here and there still in the attitudes of intimacy, emptiness and silence where there had been crowds, music and laughter. Everyone had gone home but Gene Halford, who was standing in the hall talking to the manager.

"I'm sorry to hear about this," Halford said to me.

"We all are. Where are you spending the night?"

"I've been assigned to a BOQ out at the yard, but I haven't figured out how I'm going to get there. I didn't go on the bus because I thought I should wait for you." Curiosity, excitement and pity mingled incongruously in his murky green eyes.

"What the hell, come with us," Cram said viciously. "The wagon holds seven, and I'll make everything right by joining the Drivers' Association in the morning. My name's Cram. Detective Cram."

"Halford's my name. Are you investigating this murder?"

"I wouldn't know."

"You're a lucky man, Mr. Cram, to be able to feel so casual about things."

"I mean I don't know whether it's a murder," Cram snapped. "Do you?"

"When women commit suicide they don't usually hang

30

themselves," Halford said dogmatically. "Unless of course they have a reason for wanting to look ugly after they die." His eyes in quick malice flicked toward and away from Eric's face. "Love isn't stronger than death, but vanity is."

Eric was too remote to be hurt, and didn't hear him. His pale eyes were set like stones, mesmerized by the ruined body which he had seen on the floor, blinded to everything else by grief and shame.

"Hold your tongue," I said to Halford, "or I'll run a ring through it."

His laughter was quite jolly and extremely hideous.

3

I WOKE UP and looked at my wristwatch, which said five o'clock. For a moment I lay tense and empty, waiting for the General Quarters bell to sound. Then I realized, but without relaxing, that I was in the upper bunk in Eric's stateroom on a ship in Pearl Harbor, where no enemy would strike again for a very long time. But I did not relax. There are things more terrible to the imagination than Kamikaze planes, and my imagination had lain prostrate among those things all night.

I noticed that a light was burning in the cabin, and rolled over to the edge of the berth and looked down. Eric was sitting in the steel chair in front of the steel desk, his feet wide apart on the steel deck. He hadn't undressed, and his sloping back looked immobile and infinitely tired, as if he had been sitting there all night.

But his voice was quite natural when he turned at the sound of my movement. "Go back to sleep, Sam, it's pretty early. Does this light bother you?"

"No, but the idea of you sitting there bothers me. Why don't you hit the sack?"

"I tried to but I couldn't sleep." He stood up and lit a cigarette quickly and steadily. His movements had the febrile vitality of confirmed and accepted insomnia. Watching him I had the feeling that sleep was a daily miracle, the fulfillment of a kind of faith given to idiots, children, and the blissfully drunk. And I knew that I couldn't sleep any more either.

"Cuchulain the Hound of Ulster," I said, "when tired out by wounds and battle, didn't go and take a rest like ordinary people. He went off some place and exercised to beat the band."

"Was it good for him?" Eric said. A smile shone strangely on his pale face.

"Eventually he went nuts." I swung my legs over the edge of the berth and jumped down. Eric kicked the other chair in my direction and handed me a cigarette.

"If you're concerned about me, you needn't be," he said. "I'm too goddamn selfish and practical to go nuts, or even be slightly indiscreet."

"It strikes me you've achieved indiscretion at least. But if you think I battled my way out of the arms of Morpheus to discuss your personality, you're wrong. I'd much rather tell you more about Cuchulain. Stevie Smith has a good verse about him—"

"Don't digress. I was thinking about what happened to Sue."

"All right," I said. "We'll talk about Sue Sholto. Then maybe in a couple of days or a couple of weeks we can get around to talking about your wife."

"My wife has nothing to do with this," he said monotonously, like a man repeating an incantation. "I hope to God she never hears of it."

"She will, though. You'll tell her yourself, Eric. You're the kind of a guy who'll go to her for comfort, and she's the kind of a woman who'll give it to you. That's why you married her, and that's why you'll never leave her."

"Won't I?" He smiled mirthlessly. "If I had known Sue would do what she did—"

"So you've got it all figured out. She killed herself because she couldn't have you. There may be a good deal of vanity behind your theory, you know. You've got a strong feeling of guilt about the affair, and your rationalization of the guilt leads you to the conclusion that Sue killed herself for you. You feel guilty, therefore you are."

"I appreciate your intentions. They're good enough to pave hell with. But you can't change facts with words."

"What facts? You don't know that Sue committed suicide. She may have been murdered. Halford thinks she was."

"Murdered? Who would want to murder Sue?"

"I don't know. Detective Cram doesn't know. Do you?"

"It's an incredible idea." He had nerved himself to live with the idea of her suicide, but the suggestion of murder attacked him from an unexpected quarter, struck him in a new and vulnerable place.

"Murder is always incredible," I said. "That's why it's a crime and punishable with death. But it happens. Maybe it happened last night."

"You're not taken in by that story about Hector Land, are you? That was evil nonsense. Land's a queer duck, but sexual crime isn't in his line at all."

"The crime wasn't sexual. Savo proved that. A queer duck in what way?"

"I don't know much about him actually. I intend to find out more. But he's been insubordinate on one or two occasions, been up for Captain's Mast and gotten extra duty, and so on. From some things he's said, I suspect he's pretty strong on racial feeling. Nothing revolutionary or subversive, I don't suppose, but he's not a very soothing influence on the other stewards. I have an idea, too, that he's one of the leading spirits behind the gambling pools that the black boys have—"

"Not just the black boys. I haven't met a Navy man yet that didn't gamble. Or an Army man, or a Marine."

"I know, but you have to watch it, or it gets too big. There are a lot of things you have to watch, even if you can't hope to enforce Navy Regs to the letter. Navy Regs says no gambling on USN ships, which we interpret to mean not too much gambling, and in the proper places at the proper times. I'm going to check up on everything Hector Land has done since he came aboard this ship."

There was the slap-slap of slippers in the passage, and a shadow moved across the grey fireproof curtain which hung in the hatchway. Water gurgled in the scuttlebutt outside, and then the curtain was thrust aside to admit a tousled sandy head and a naked tanned shoulder. The head had a square face and small humorous eyes.

"Hello, Eric," the head said in a Texas drawl, wiping its

34

wet mouth with the hairy back of a hand. "Get up early to nurse your hangover?"

"Walked the floor with it all night. You haven't met Will, have you, Sam? He's our Communications Officer. Ensign Drake, Lieutenant Wolson."

"Glad to know you, Drake. Communications Officer, Chief Censor, Public Relations Officer, general handyman, and convenient scapegoat. And the rest of the wardroom bitches like hell because I don't stand deck watches in my spare time. I didn't even get to the party last night—the Captain wanted to get off a message. Now he wants to get off another message, not that it couldn't wait until we get to Diego—"

"It's definite, then, is it?" Eric said. "We're going to have our availability in San Diego?"

"It sure looks like it, but you never can tell in the Navy. Don't spread it around, or a lot of people may be disappointed."

"You didn't miss much last night," I said to Wolson. "The party started out with a bang but it ended up with a whimper."

"I heard about that. It was tough on Eric. What's the word on that deal? I heard you mention Hector Land before I looked in."

"I've got to check up on him," Eric said. "He was seen coming out of the room where—where the thing happened. I was convinced it was suicide, but now I'm not so sure."

"You knew the girl, didn't you?" Curiosity bubbled behind Wolson's narrow impassive stare.

"She was a friend," Eric said coldly.

On shipboard even more than on shore, you can't afford to be too interested in the other fellow's business or you risk making enemies. Wolson changed the subject:

"While you're checking up on Land, you might ask him where he gets all the money he's been sending home. He must have mailed his wife five hundred dollars in the last couple of months—"

"He did?" Eric stood up. "Have you got a record of that?"

35

"Naturally. We log all enclosures in the letters we censor, more to protect ourselves than anything else."

"I'd like to see your book. It would take Land at least a year to save five hundred dollars out of his pay."

"How about now? I'm going up to the Comm Office as soon as I get dressed."

A few minutes later we followed Wolson up three ladders to the Communications Office, where he handed us his clothbound logbook. "You'll have to pick out the entries yourself," he said to Eric. "The Captain's been calling for me again."

Wolson hurried off to the Captain's cabin, and Eric and I sat down with the book. He looked up the entries and I wrote them down in a column on a slip of paper. In twenty minutes we found the record of six enclosures in letters which Hector Land had sent to Mrs. Hector Land in Detroit. The entries, which were dated, extended over the last three months. Each was for approximately one hundred dollars, and the total was six hundred and twenty dollars.

"He didn't save that out of his Navy pay," Eric said. "He's got another source of income."

"Gambling?"

"Could be. He'd have to have a wonderful run of luck."

"He could have won it all at once, in one glorious crapgame, and sent it home in installments to avoid suspicion."

"That's true. The dates correspond with the times we've been in port. We've been in and out of Pearl regularly for the last three months. We've been in for three or four days approximately every two weeks. Of course he had to send it off when we were in port, because you can't mail letters at sea. I wonder where in hell he got his money."

"Where's Land now?"

"In his quarters, I suppose. He's restricted to the ship until the next Captain's Mast, and then he'll probably get the brig."

"For what?"

"He admitted himself that he went into that room to

36

steal whiskey. Even if that's the only thing he did, he's in for it and he knows it."

"I don't suppose we'll get anything out of him this morning," I said. "Last night scared him stiff. But I think we should have a talk with him."

"I think so too."

We found Land in the wardroom helping another steward to set the tables for breakfast. He avoided looking at us and went on working as if we weren't there. He worked quickly and intently as if he would willingly devote his whole life and all his faculties to the safe and homely task of unfolding tablecloths and arranging knives and forks and spoons.

When Eric called, "Land!" he straightened up and said, "Yessir," still without looking at us. In the bright iron room his scarred black face and huge torso looked incongruous and lost, like a forest tree torn from its roots by a storm or a flood and lodged in an alien and fatal place.

"Come here and sit down," Eric said. "I want to talk to you for a minute."

He moved toward us quickly, and, after we had seated ourselves, sat down on the edge of a chair. "Yessir?"

"You've been sending a good deal of money home lately."

"Not so much, sir. Just what I manage to save. My wife needs the money, sir."

"No doubt she does. But that doesn't explain where you've been getting it."

"I saved it, sir. I hardly spend any money on myself at all. I send her all my pay, sir."

"Where did you get six hundred and seventy dollars in the last three months? If you stall, I'll know you're lying."

Land's jaws moved convulsively, in labor with an answer, but no words came. Finally he said: "I made it, sir. I just made it."

"How?"

"I made it gambling. I'm powerfully lucky with the dice, and I made that money gambling."

"Who with?"

"Just with the boys. Anybody that wanted to play."

"Men from this ship?"

"Yessir. Well, no, sir. Some of them was I guess. I don't remember."

"Think about it, and remember, Land. Because I'm going to check up on your story, and if you're lying it's going to be too bad for you. You're in a pretty bad position as it is, and this gambling deal isn't going to help."

"Yessir," Land said, the muscles of his face tense with repressed fear. "I made the money gambling. That's the truth, and that's why I'm telling you. I'm a lucky man at craps—"

"That's what you said. Go out in the galley and see if there's any chow for us. It's nearly time for breakfast."

Land rose as if a spring had been released under him, and almost ran into the galley.

"Do you think he's telling the truth?"

"How should I know?" Eric said a little snappily. "A black never tells the truth to a white if he can think of anything better. He's got too much to lose."

A loudspeaker on the bulkhead began to rasp: "Lieutenant Swann please lay down to the quarterdeck for a telephone call. Telephone call on the quarterdeck for—"

"It's probably the police," Eric said wearily. "What was that detective's name?"

"Cram."

It was Detective Cram calling from Honolulu. He wanted to get formal statements from Eric and me, concerning the circumstances of Sue Sholto's death and my discovery of the body.

"He wants to talk to you," Eric said when he had told me this.

I took the receiver and said, "Drake speaking."

"This is Cram. Can you come over to police headquarters this morning? I want to get your story straight."

"Yes, but I have to report in at the Transport Office first. I may have to leave on pretty short notice."

"Yeah, I know. We're going to have the inquest this

38

afternoon. You'll have to be there, also Lieutenant Swann."

"We'll be there. Are there any new developments?"

"No, but the coroner has his doubts about it being a suicide. The trouble is, we've got no lead. Anybody could have done it, including the deceased. The whole thing's wide open, and I don't know how we're going to get it closed. Do you?"

"No."

"Well, we'll talk about it when you come over to my office. Nine o'clock suit you?"

"Right."

We talked about it for nearly two hours behind the Venetian blinds in Cram's office, and got nowhere. Sue Sholto could have been killed by Land, by Eric, by me, by Gene Halford, by Mary Thompson, by Mrs. Merriwell, by Dr. Savo, by any one of a hundred people. No one who was at the party could account for his actions continuously, and there wasn't even any reason for limiting the field of suspects to those who had attended the party. Honolulu House had been wide open to anyone all evening.

The stubborn fact that always stymied us, the blind alley where each new idea led, was that no one had any apparent reason for killing Sue. Eric and Mary were the only ones with whom Sue had had any personal relations, so far as we knew, and neither of them seemed an eligible suspect. I was not surprised that the upshot of the inquest, like the conclusion of our morning's talk, was the verdict that Sue Sholto had died by her own hand.

During the inquest, which was repetitious, dull, and obscure, I watched Mary. She was the only object in the bare, sweltering room on which the eyes could rest without effort. She showed the effects of her friend's death, of course; in the luminous pallor of her skin, the mournful directness of her gaze, the intense stillness of her hands when she gave her testimony. Once or twice her voice broke when she described Sue's usual gaiety, contrasting with her sudden and unaccountable depression the night before.

"Yet I didn't think it was a suicidal depression," Mary said in answer to the Coroner's question. "Sue was deeply emotional, passionate, but she never gave way to anything like—such black despair." Her eyes grew dark with horror of the image that her imagination saw: a lithe body twisted and limp, a bright face become sodden and blue, a discontent with life so great that it preferred nothing. Mary had difficulty in speaking, and the Coroner excused her from the witness stand.

When the inquest was over Mary was the first to leave the room, walking quickly and blindly to the door. But when I made my way to the hall she was there waiting for me.

"I hoped I'd have a chance to talk to you before you left," she said.

"I was going to call you if we didn't. I go out tomorrow."

"Tomorrow? That's very soon."

"Not too soon for me. Hawaii's going to have a funny taste for me from now on."

"For me too. I'm beginning to feel that nothing good can happen here. There's something ominous and anti-human about those mountains, and the clouds, and the bright green sea, and a climate that's too good all the time."

"Something good can happen here." I was impressed by her feelings but unwilling to be carried away by them. "If you'll have dinner with me."

"I'm afraid I'm not very cheerful company. But I'd like to."

"I think we should try to forget the whole business for a while. What do you say to driving up to the north shore for a swim? I can get a jeep from the Transportation Center."

"I'd have to go home and change, and get my swimming-suit."

When I picked her up she had changed to white linen, and a bandana for her hair. Then we drove across the island. It was warmer inland, but the wind blew freshly in the open sides of the jeep and whipped the color into her cheeks. The air was suffused with light, the tender green

of the young pineapple shoots was like a whispered promise in the fields, the palmtrunks rose straight towards the
sun like a high song. But here and there along the road,
more frequently as we went higher, there were ribs and
boulders of volcanic rock, as if hell had thrust a shoulder
through the earth.

By tacit agreement we avoided talking of Sue's death.
In fact we did very little talking at all, saving our breath
for swimming and running. There was no reef to break
the surf, and it came into the white beach high and
strong, as hard to ride and as exciting as a mettlesome
horse. Mary was like a porpoise in the waves. She forgot
her earlier depression, and lived in her senses like a young
animal.

When we were tired out we lay in the clean coarse
sand, and she slept while I watched her. I watched her
smooth shoulders, her honey-colored hair curled in the
nape of her neck, her round arms, her long brown thighs,
the delicate decline and fullness of her back and buttocks.
I didn't touch her or speak to her, but I memorized her
body.

Only after night fell was there a recurrence of her
unhappy mood. We were walking on the beach below the
inn where we had eaten dinner. The evening breeze was
beginning to blow in from the disappearing sea. The half-
visible breakers, approaching and receding, kept up a
muttering which rose and fell like a sad native chant.

"I'm cold," Mary said. She shivered slightly against my
arm. "And I'm afraid."

"What you need is another drink. Or maybe two."

"Ten would do the trick, I guess. But that would only
postpone it until tomorrow."

"Postpone what?"

"The way I feel. I feel awfully bleak and desolate,
and frightened. I hate this island, Sam. I have a feeling
that something terrible will happen if I stay here."

"Something terrible has happened, but not to you. It's a
selfish way to look at it, but I've seen men die, and the
pity and terror are always alleviated by the fact that it

41

isn't one's self. The war develops scar tissue in everyone's sensibilities."

"Surely the war has nothing to do with this. Has it?"

"I was explaining my point of view. But I don't know. Remember what Gene Halford said about enemy agents in these islands? It was about then that Sue's mood changed, and soon after that she—she died. It's barely possible, isn't it, that there's a connection?"

"Don't say that, please. You're frightening me more."

We were standing facing each other now, all by ourselves in a remote corner of the dim and deserted beach. I moved closer to look into her face. Her eyes were dark as the night sky, and her mouth was an anguished dark-red gash, tremulous and pitiable.

"Why are you afraid?" I said. "I don't get it. Unless you had the same idea."

"What idea?"

"The idea that Sue's death was connected with the war. Did you?"

"No, not exactly. But we worked in the same place, and did the same things. If she was killed, whoever, or whatever, killed her may try to kill me too. I know I must sound childish, but I'm afraid."

"That's what you said before, but I don't see any reason for it. Unless you know more about it than I do?"

"No, I don't. I don't. That's what makes it so terrible. The whole thing has no reason to it."

"All right, if you're afraid, why don't you leave the island? Go back to your folks in the States. Oahu gets some people down, and you seem to be one of them."

"I am going," she said softly and firmly. "I couldn't go on in the station without Sue, anyway. I resigned this morning."

"It'll be a blow to the station to lose both of you at once."

"Do you think I'm a welcher?"

"Hell," I said. "People have to work out their own lives. If Oahu frightens you, obviously you have to leave it."

Far down the shore to our left as we turned seaward there was the chatter and crash of guns. Mary moved against me and I put my arm around her shoulders, feeling the tiny vibration of the nerves throughout her body.

"It's nothing," I said. "They have anti-aircraft practice out here nearly every night."

The tracers were rising into the sky like luminous juggler's balls in gentle and terrific flight. The tempo of the guns increased, rising in a raucous crescendo. The long white gaze of searchlights began to scan the empty blackness, crossing and intertwining like desperate searching fingers.

Mary turned inwards to me as my other arm went around her waist. "Kiss me," she said.

We stood interlocked, dizzy and warm, under the zebra-striped sky, until the sound of the guns and the beating of our hearts were a single clamor.

PART II

DETROIT

4

FIVE thousand miles and two weeks later I met Mary again. It was not a coincidence. We had known each other for only a little more than twenty-four hours, but neither of us was willing to let it end there. Before we parted that night in Hawaii, we exchanged Stateside addresses and telephone numbers.

I had kept on my bachelor apartment in Detroit by subletting it to a friend. When I got home I moved in with him. During my first week in Detroit not much happened to me externally but a good deal happened inside. I went to visit my old girl-friend Sandra, and found that she had flown the coop. She was in Florida with her very new husband, a very new flier stationed at Pensacola. The thought of Mary cushioned the blow, and I was surprised at how little I cared.

I was content to lead a bachelor life with my sub-tenant, a reporter on a morning paper named Joe Scott. I did a good deal of sitting around catching up on my reading and my drinking. The drinking was mostly beer and in the evenings, because I had nothing to escape from and was where I wanted to be. I went to a few shows and one or two parties, where I found myself mostly among acquaintances, not friends. Nearly all my friends were in the services, or in Washington, or in the OWI overseas. Still, it was good to be home for twenty days. Before the week was up I had begun to wonder how I could ever bring myself to go back out to the Pacific. I felt half like a civilian again, and even when I was bored it was good to be bored by something different from sea and sun and bogies on the radar screen.

With the war, Sue Sholto's death receded like a nightmare in the morning. More vivid and frequent in my memory was Mary's long brown body in the sand, the freshness of her mouth, the way she held me on the last night. The bad business came back and hit me hardest the day before Mary telephoned. I went to Ann Arbor to make a duty call on Eric Swann's wife.

I had put it off for a week and couldn't very well put it off any longer. I was embarrassed for Eric's sake, though I had no objective reason to be. The story of Sue's death had gone no further than the local Hawaiian press. Eric had been mentioned only in passing, as a member of the party who had testified at the inquest. Still I felt embarrassment, which deepened in the face of the woman's love and loyalty to her husband.

Helen Swann was a big pale blonde, vaguely warm and vaguely nervous, the antithesis of Sue Sholto. She was the *hausfrau* type, but childless, so that all her love was lavished on her husband.

"You saw Eric, didn't you?" she said in an eager flutter, when she had perfunctorily praised my tan and the lucky stars which had brought me back. "He wrote me about it. Tell me, is he well?"

"He seemed very well when I saw him in Pearl," I lied. "In tip-top form."

"I'm so glad. You know, he always tells me in his letters how well he's feeling, but I can't entirely believe him. It's so nice to have confirmation. You see, even if he were sick he wouldn't tell me, he wouldn't want to worry me, the poor dear."

"You'll be able to see for yourself," I said, wondering how deep her loving eyes would see. "His ship's coming back to the States."

"I know," she said, her soft mouth wreathed in a girlish smile which struck a pang through me. "He's coming home tomorrow. Look."

With the air of a magician solving the riddle of time and space, she picked up a yellow telegram from the table and gave it to me to read:

"Isn't it wonderful?" she said. "I don't care how short the time is if only I can see him again. And he's coming tomorrow."

"That's swell," but my enthusiasm rang a little uncertainly in my ears. I doubted Eric's ability to shift with perfect ease from a dead mistress to a living wife. On the other hand, Helen Swann's tremulous and brooding love needed very little to feed on. Which was why, I thought, her husband had been unfaithful to her.

I stayed long enough to satisfy propriety if not all her eager questions, and promised to have dinner with them during Eric's leave. Then I went back to Detroit to read a book and forget about women.

The next morning Mary Thompson telephoned from Cleveland. As soon as I heard her low rich voice I knew what had been keeping me dull and somnolent all week. It was suppressed expectation, suppressed by the fear that I'd never hear from her again.

"You made it fast," I said. "I'm damn glad."

"Fast for a civilian. I'm damn glad too. How long have you been home?"

"A week."

"Having a good time?"

"In a quiet way. I suddenly realized when I heard your voice that I've been waiting very hard to hear from you."

"That's nice. If you mean it. You're sure you're not really put out to hear from me, and just carrying it off like a gentleman?"

"You know different. My feeling for you is not precisely gentlemanly. When can I see you?"

"Well, I'm coming back to Detroit today. Not to see you: it's about a job."

"Back to Detroit? You mean you were here and didn't call me?"

"I was just passing through from Chicago. I had to come here to see the folks. Not that any explanation is called for. Avoid that proprietary tone." Her voice was mocking, but a little steel grated in it. "How's the girl-friend?"

"Married off, thank God. In which case will you meet me for dinner at the Book-Cadillac at eight?"

"I'd love to. See you." She hung up.

A couple of hours later I had another telephone call, and I began to feel as if it were Pearl Harbor old home week. This time it was Eric, calling from the airport.

"I'm glad I could get in touch with you," he said when we had exchanged greetings. "Something new has been added."

"In connection with—it?"

"Not exactly. Perhaps. Hector Land has disappeared."

"I thought he was in the brig."

"He was for ten days. Then we let him out, but he was restricted to the ship. The night we got into Diego he got away somehow, and hasn't been seen since."

"I don't see how he got out of the Yard."

"We weren't in the Yard yet. We docked at North Island when we came in. I figure he must have slipped over the side and swum around to one of the unrestricted beaches, maybe at Coronado. He may have drowned himself, for that matter. Anyway he's gone."

"His being A.W.O.L. doesn't prove very much, does it?"

"Not much. But I'm still interested in checking up on him. That's the main reason I called you. His wife lives in Detroit."

"I know. Somewhere in Paradise Valley."

"I can't take the time now—Helen will be waiting for me—but I thought I'd come into town tonight and look up Mrs. Land. Are you free?"

"Sorry," I said. "I have a dinner engagement."

"Could we get together afterwards?"

For a moment I thought of asking him to leave me out of it, let me forget it even if he couldn't. But I said: "Look, it's Mary Thompson I'm having dinner with—she just got back to the States. Why don't you bring Helen and make it a foursome? We'll make a night of it and if we get the chance we'll look up Mrs. Land."

As soon as I made the suggestion I regretted it. There are more entertaining projects for a mixed group than looking in Paradise Valley for a Negro woman you have never seen. Apart from that, I anticipated a certain amount of strain in a meeting between Eric's wife and Sue's friend. But Eric took me up on it and the engagement was made for eight.

The party fitted together better than I expected. Helen was so delighted to be with Eric again that nothing could have phased her, and Eric flourished in the atmosphere of devotion which she generated. Mary, who I remembered had understood Eric from the beginning, was content to let well enough alone. She made no mention of Sue, nor even any subtly feminine insinuation, and the two women were soon on their way to becoming friends.

Mary had changed noticeably since I had seen her. On Oahu her whole nature had seemed open, like a rose in a sudden hailstorm, to the shock and pain of events. She had been shaken by the vibration of horror which had passed through Honolulu House, and I had felt helpless to comfort her, though I did my best. Now she seemed no longer vulnerable. Her nature had closed upon itself and become poised and self-contained again. Perhaps it was no more than the healthful effects of putting the island and its associations behind her, of taking a sea-voyage, of coming home again. But she seemed a different woman.

The difference was emphasized by the Martinis and highballs we had before and after dinner. When Eric and I proposed our expedition, Mary took it up with sophomore enthusiasm:

"I think it should be fun. A manhunt through the wilds of Detroit. A womanhunt, at least."

"Hardly that," Eric said drily. "I've got her address. 214 Chestnut Street."

Helen was a bit put out: "I thought you were on leave, Eric. You've only got five days and one day's gone already."

He looked a little sheepish but said: "This won't take half an hour. After that we'll hit the night-spots."

Mary and I shared the back seat of Eric's carefully

51

preserved sedan, and I lost interest in where we were going. She let me kiss her, but her mouth was not tremulous and yielding as it had been the one other time. She kissed me firmly back.

Before I wanted to see it I saw the number 214 in rusty metal nailed above the door of a dark building. It stood among other buildings like it, huge multicellular mansions which had once housed a single family in rather stuffy luxury, and now housed twenty or more. Hemmed in by economic pressure and social injustice, the Negroes swarmed in the rotting hives which they had neither built nor chosen, three, five, or seven to a room. The old houses were eaten away by interior decay, the plumbing dissolved and went away in the sewers, the floors and walls were unpainted and unpapered, the roofs were sagging and porous, the heating systems were left unused or taken out to be sold as scrap metal; and the landlords made no repairs, because they were not needed to rent the buildings. Yet from the outside, especially when snow and bleak weather kept the tenants huddled inside around their stoves, the houses looked as they had always looked. Their façades were ornate and imposing, like a pompous matron with a social disease.

Mary wanted to go in with us, for the adventure, she said, but Helen was glad enough to stay outside of the gloomy building.

"This isn't a very good section," Eric said, apparently regretting the impulse which had made him bring his wife here. "Keep the doors locked, and if anybody tries to bother you just drive around the block."

We left them bundled up in their furs in the front seat, and knocked on the door of the silent house. A glass window set high in the huge carved door was painted over and shone whitely like an eye blinded by cataract. We knocked again, and when nobody answered opened the door and entered the dark hallway. The hall was deserted, but it was odorous and murmurous, alive with the memories and promises of human life: cooking and eating, copulation and birth, quarrels and music and violence.

The first door to the right showed a crack of light. I knocked on it and the crack widened.

"Who you want?" said the half-face, leathery and wrinkled and crowned with a grey poll, which appeared in the lighted crack.

"Does Mrs. Hector Land live here?"

"Bessie Land live down the hall," the old man said impatiently. "Third to the left." He shut the door.

We stepped carefully among perambulators and empty milkbottles and found the door. I lit my lighter and found a card nailed to the door with a thumbtack. It bore two autographs: Mrs. Bessie Land, Mrs. Kate Morgan.

I knocked on the door and a woman shouted brusquely: "Go away, I'm busy."

There were sounds from inside the room which indicated the nature of the business.

"I don't like this," Eric said suddenly. "Let's get out of here."

I said: "Did you expect Mrs. Land to receive you in her drawing-room with her best tiara on?"

I knocked again and the sounds ceased. A young Negro woman came to the door holding a cotton wrapper across her breast. She kicked without malice at a white mongrel puppy which bounded out of the darkness and nipped at her slippers.

"Mrs. Hector Land?" I said.

"Bessie ain't here. She ain't in business any more anyway. If you wait a few minutes, maybe I—?"

She raised her right hand to stroke back her hair and made her right breast rise under the wrapper.

"We came to see Mrs. Land," Eric said hastily. "On business. That is, not—." He blushed and subsided.

"Suits me," the black girl said, and smiled without warmth. "I'm tired tonight. Bessie's over at the Paris Bar and Grill. Around the corner to your left."

We found Helen and Mary shivering in the car in spite of heater and furs, and drove around the corner to the left. A gap-toothed neon in red and orange flickered on the dirty snow like a dying fire, proclaiming the Paris Bar and Grill.

53

"Better come in and have a drink," I said to Mary. "It's cold out here."

"Are you quite sure it's safe?" Helen said. "It looks like an all-Negro place."

"So what?" I said. "This is a democracy, isn't it? They drink the same liquor we do, and it makes them drunk just like us."

"Come on," Mary said, and we all went in. There was a lunch-counter along the left wall, along the right a row of booths with tall thin partitions between them, and a bar at the back. At the right end of the bar there was a boogie-woogie piano with a black boogie-woogie pianist playing it. The big room was loud with the intricate rustle and jangle of boogie-woogie, thick with smoke, and crowded with people. But there wasn't much talking, and there was no laughter. I realized with a jolt that everyone in the room was conscious of our presence. I was embarrassed by the power of my skin to stop a roomful of conversations. Our progress down the room was a little like running a moral gauntlet.

All the booths were full but there was room at the bar for us. We sat down and asked the bartender for four bourbons and the whereabouts of Mrs. Hector Land.

"Right beside you," he said to me with a smile. I looked at the woman beside me. She was black but comely, like the girl in Song of Songs: well-made, with strong delicate lines in her face and long narrow eyes. But her eyes weren't very well focussed and her mouth was gloomy and slack. There was a little glass of brownish fluid in front of her.

"Mrs. Land?" I said.

"Yes." I smelt wormwood on her breath.

"I'm Ensign Drake. This is Lieutenant Swann, who would like to ask you a question or two."

"Questions about what?" she said drowsily. Her eyes swung in her head slowly as if by their own weight.

"About your husband."

"You know Hector? Why yes, you're a Navy officer, aren't you? He's in the Navy." Eric was standing by her shoulder now. She turned on her stool to look up at him, resting her cheek on one hand. Her elbow overturned the glass in front of her.

"Damn," she said without feeling. "Another one, Bob."

"Haven't you had about enough, Bessie?"

"That's what you always say. When do I ever get enough? Give me another one, Bob."

He shrugged his shoulders and filled a fresh glass for her. Mrs. Land paid him out of a black leather bag.

Mary, who had missed nothing, didn't miss the bag. "That's good leather," she said to me in a whisper. "Her clothes are good, too. Why on earth does she live like this?"

"Too much drinking can explain anything," I said. "But it requires explanation in turn."

"There's a reason for everything, including drunkenness, I suppose."

"She isn't so drunk."

"Don't kid yourself," Mary said, so loudly that the bartender cocked an ear. "I know females and female drunkenness, and she's so drunk that you'll get no sense out of her. We might as well go home."

"The young lady's right," the bartender leaned over the bar to say confidentially to me. "Bessie's here every night and never leaves till we close the bar at midnight. She can take an awful lot, but not when she drinks absinthe. It puts you to sleep, see?"

I looked and saw. She breathed slowly and heavily like a patient in anaesthesia. Her movements were sluggish and uncertain. Her eyes were clouded.

"So Hector ran away from the Navy, eh?" she was saying. She laughed a laugh which descended the scale and died in a groan. "He always said he'd do it when the time came. Ever since he joined Black Israel."

A tall man in a tan fedora and overcoat who was sitting on her other side leaned towards her and said through thin purple lips: "You're talking a lot of crap, Bessie. Hector wouldn't like that, would he?"

She straightened, and the last curves of laughter were smoothed out of her face. The piano-player began Suitcase Blues, and surprisingly she started to hum with the music

55

in an alcoholic contralto. Before the song ended there were tears rolling down her cheeks, and when it did she put her head down on her arms and sobbed. Her glass rolled off the bar and crashed on the floor.

Eric said to her back: "I'll come and see you tomorrow."

"Don't you think she should be gotten out of here?" I said to the bartender. "We'll take her home if necessary."

"She's all right if you don't try to talk to her," he said coldly. "Try to get her out of here before midnight and she fight like a wildcat."

"You will not come and see her tomorrow," Helen Swann was saying to Eric. "You'll stay in your own home for at least one day of your leave, I hope. And for God's sake let's get out of here and back to civilzation," she concluded petulantly.

Civilization consisted of paying three times as much for our drinks and listening to the same kind of music played worse. After I agreed to go and see Mrs. Land the next day instead of Eric, Helen began to enjoy herself again, but Mary didn't. We were in a smoke-filled basement, the most crowded because the most popular place in town, and it didn't agree with Mary. After a couple of drinks she asked me to take her home.

"I'm sorry, Sam," she said in the taxi with her head on my shoulder. "It's the migraine again, and there's nothing I can do about it except go to bed. The doctor said I'll never get over it till I learn to face things I don't like."

"I'm sorrier. We shouldn't have taken you to Paradise Valley. It was pretty depressing, wasn't it?"

"We'll paint the town red another night, eh?"

"Tomorrow?"

"I'd love to," she said in a tired little-girl voice.

She left me in the lobby of her hotel and the elevator took her away. I felt depressed, partly because the evening had petered out but mostly because I felt responsible for Mary's loss of spirits. I walked to the nearest bar and downed three double whiskies in the half-hour before closing-time. Then I walked home and went to bed.

My tenant Joe Scott usually worked on his paper till

two or three in the morning, and slept until noon. He wasn't in yet when I went to bed, and when I got up he was still sleeping. Though there was something I wanted to ask him, I decided not to wake him. Perhaps after a good night's sleep Bessie Land herself would be willing and able to tell me what Black Israel was.

Bessie Land might have been willing, but she was not able.

I took a taxi to Chestnut Street and alighted at the corner within sight of the Paris Bar and Grill. The neon sign was out, and under the light snow which had fallen during the night the streets looked peaceful and deserted. The snow was heel-packed on the sidewalks where the early risers had beaten their path to work, but it was after nine o'clock now and there was no one in sight.

I raised my overcoat collar against the bitter gusts which whirled the snow between the buildings, and made my way to 214 Chestnut. Inside the tenement there were the sounds of morning life: babies crying and crowing, children playing, women's voices raised in gossip and argument. But the hallway was cold and empty, and all the doors were closed to conserve the heat in the rooms. The third door to the left was closed like the others, and I knocked on it and waited. I might have waited forever if I hadn't turned the knob and gone in.

Bessie Land was flat on her back on the bed, staring at the discolored ceiling. One arm hung over the edge of the bed so that the hand half-rested on the floor. From the hand spread a pool of blood. The white mongrel puppy huddled there, licking the bloody hand.

When I moved nearer, the dog crawled under the bed. I saw that Bessie Land's throat was deeply cut. The pull of the skin had made a raw ellipse in her darkly glistening neck. A wavy-edged bread-knife rested on the quilt beside her head. She had her coat on, but it did not prevent her from being terribly cold.

5

THREE minutes after I entered my call at the pay phone in the hall, a police siren whooped in the distance. Another thirty seconds and it howled like a wolf in the street. Suddenly it stopped, as if somebody had shot it.

A police lieutenant in a blue uniform and a man in civilian clothes came down the hall toward me with the air of men going to work.

"My name's Cassettari," the Lieutenant said. "You didn't touch anything, like I said?"

"Not a thing. That is, I touched her face to see if she was cold. She's very cold."

The man in civilian clothes, a middle-aged man with grey hair and a frosty bitter face, examined the body without disturbing it. "You said it, she's cold," he said. "Fast-frozen nigger wench. Any necrophiles around, might be a market."

"How long's she been dead, Doc?" Cassettari said. He had a fleshy Mediterranean face. A thick dead cigar made the right side of his mouth sneer continuously. He used the cigar instead of a finger to point at things. His fingers were busy holding his hips.

"Eight-nine hours. I'll know better when I get her stomach out, if there's any of it left after the liquor she's been drinking. But take a look at the postmortem lividity."

I took a look. The hanging arm was heavy with stagnant blood.

"Did she kill herself?" Cassettari said.

"Fingerprints should tell. Where the hell's Randy?"

"He'll be along. He had to pack his kit."

After a minute or two, the doctor said: "Yeah, she killed

58

herself. There's a hesitation mark." He pointed a casual finger at the slashed throat. I saw the shallow cut above and parallel to the deep wound. "You don't get a hesitation mark when a buck nigger cuts his whore."

I said: "There's more to this case than a buck nigger cutting a whore." I told them briefly why I thought so.

"He's been reading *The Shadow*," Cassettari said.

"He's been reading Dick Tracy, too," Doc said.

"This woman was murdered," I said.

"This woman was murdered, he says," Doc said. "If she was murdered it's our business to find out."

"I wouldn't be meddling in your business if you showed any sign of knowing it."

"Wait till you see a few more bodies," Doc said. "You won't go off the deep end every time you see one. I wonder where the hell Randy is."

"If you won't listen to me, I'll find somebody who will."

"He's going to bring pressure to bear," Cassettari said.

"Listen, son," Doc said. "These niggers get bumped every day. This woman killed herself. Hesitation marks mean suicide, understand? You're not in your field."

I said: "Maybe you're out of your class."

"Get the hell out of here," Cassettari said. "You talk too goddamn much. Wait a minute, give me your address and phone. I suppose you got to say your piece at the inquest."

I gave him what he asked for and went away, walking on legs made stiff by anger.

After that I had to get my information about the case from the newspapers, and from Joe Scott. His paper was the tabloid type, and intended to give the case a play. (Next day I saw what they did with it: Navy Wife Suicides at Husband's Desertion.) He told me that the bread knife which had cut Bessie's throat bore only her own fingerprints, and those of Mrs. Kate Morgan. Kate Morgan pointed out that naturally her prints were on the knife, she used it for cutting bread. She was shocked and grieved by her roommate's death, and besides she had a perfect alibi. A considerable time before midnight, when Bessie left the

Paris Bar and Grill, Mrs. Kate Morgan had received a telephone call and had immediately gone to spend the night with a certain gentleman in a certain hotel. When she got home the police were there.

Joe was interested in what Bessie Land had said about Black Israel, but didn't know any more about it than I did. He stroked his long sharp nose and looked thoughtfully over his lunch. "You might try Wanless," he said finally. "It sounds like another of these Negro societies, and he knows all about 'em."

"Simeon Wanless? The sociologist?"

"That's the man. He did a pretty good book on the genesis of the race riot. It must have come out since your time."

"It must have. I know Wanless by sight, though. Is he still in Ann Arbor?"

"So far as I know."

Wanless still was. I found him two hours later in his little office in Angell Hall, which is the main building of the University of Michigan. He was sitting by himself swamped by papers, papers which were piled on his desk, on chairs, on the floor, and in the shelves which lined the walls. When I knocked on the half-open door he looked up with a smile, as if glad to have an excuse to rest his eyes.

"What can I do for you, sir?"

"My name's Drake." We shook hands and I sat down at his invitation. "I won't try to tell you the whole story, but you may be able to help me with some information."

"My sole stock in trade. Information about what?"

"I understand that you know a lot about the Negro population of Detroit."

"I've been studying them for years. A great people. You may have seen my book on the riots?"

"Not where I've been. We think we're lucky to get the pony edition of Newsmagazine the Weekly Newsmagazine."

"But that's beside the point. It's funny, isn't it, how hard it is for an author not to mention his book?"

"I was told you know a good deal about Negro social organizations. Did you ever hear of Black Israel?"

"Why, yes. I believe I have. I've heard it mentioned, that is. I was never able to get inside of it, so to speak."

"It isn't some sort of a Black Hand organization, is it?"

"Good lord, no. At least I don't think so. It's a racist organization, standing for greater equality, more rights for the Negro, and so forth. There are a good many of them."

"So far as you know, then, there's nothing criminal or sinister in Black Israel. Nothing that would lead to murder."

"I'll tell you frankly, Mr. Drake, my study has been chiefly concerned with organizations that might have had a bearing on the Detroit race riots. Black Israel wasn't active at that time, to my knowledge. When I examined the situation I found that similar racist societies among the Negroes had little or nothing to do with precipitating the riots. They were a product of many factors: economic competition and jealousy, Negro progress coming into conflict with the reactionary attitudes of Southern whites who have settled in Detroit. Attitudes which were deliberately encouraged and inflamed by certain demagogues and, in some cases, at least, by enemy agents."

I had no time to listen to a lecture, so I said: "Thank you very much. May I use your phone?"

"Certainly. I'm sorry I couldn't answer your specific question. Black Israel is rather mysterious in that it never gets in the limelight, though it may be quite important. I'd suggest that you ask some intelligent Negro what it's all about. They know what's going on among their own people."

"Thanks, I'll try that."

I took the desk phone and dialled Eric's number. When he answered I said: "Sam speaking. I'm in Ann Arbor, and I'm coming right over."

"Where are you now?"

"Angell Hall."

"I'm coming into town. Why not meet me at Davenport's?"

"Say in half an hour?" I hung up.

Davenport's is an ancient saloon and restaurant just off Main Street. I walked there and had ham on a bun and a bottle of beer while waiting for Eric. When he came in I ordered the same for him and another beer for myself. Then I noticed that he had a fresh Detroit newspaper in his hand, and a face which was partly very red and partly very white.

"Why in God's name didn't you tell me this over the phone?" he said when he'd sat down.

"Dr. Wanless was sitting beside me. I thought you mightn't want your interest in the case known."

"Yes. I see. What in hell does it mean? What sort of a thing are we mixed up in anyway?"

"That's what I wanted to talk to you about. The police are calling it suicide again. That gives us two suicides in two weeks, one on Oahu, one in Detroit. Maybe it's a coincidence that I discovered the body both times. And maybe that coincidence has me unjustifiably convinced that there's a connection between the two deaths. But by God I am convinced, and I don't think either of them was suicide."

"I don't know how you're going to tie the two together and make a case out of them. You haven't even got a real suspect."

"Hector Land was in a position to kill Sue. How many days ago did he leave the ship?"

"Let's see. Three. Four tonight."

"He could be in Detroit now. And there's another thing. Bessie Land mentioned her husband's joining Black Israel, and saying after that that he'd run away from the Navy."

"I remember," Eric said. "What is Black Israel?"

"I don't know, but I'm bloody well going to find out. The man next to her at the bar practically threatened her to make her shut up. This morning she was dead. It could be that Black Israel is a sort of *Maffia*, and Hector Land one of its thugs."

"It could be that it's as harmless as the Baptist Church. You seem to be making a great deal out of nothing at all."

"Two murders are not my idea of nothing at all. I admit that Wanless thinks Black Israel is harmless. But

62

there's one other thing, that I can't help thinking is connected with the case."

"Now what?" Eric said wearily. He ordered two more bottles of beer.

"Do you remember the conversation we had before supper the night Sue was killed?"

"How enemy agents would be able to get information out of Oahu, you mean?"

"And you remember what Gene Halford said, that information actually was leaking out? I think that Sue's death may be connected with that fact."

"I don't see how."

"She worked in a broadcasting station. She had access to means of communications—"

"What damned nonsense!" Eric exploded angrily.

"You didn't let me finish. I'm not accusing her. She could have been approached by an enemy spy with a proposition, turned it down, and been killed to keep her quiet. I can't explain the thing. All I'm trying to get at is that these deaths need more looking into. Are you with me?"

"No," Eric said stonily. "I've got a certain responsibility to my wife—"

"I know. And two days left. All right, I'll do what I can by myself."

I left Eric sitting with his half-finished bottle of beer and caught a train to Detroit. From the station I took a cab to the black town, then walked through bleak streets of slum houses, every second one of which had a service star in a window, to the Paris Bar and Grill. When I got there twilight was gathering like soot in the low sky over the icy roofs of the tenements.

The booths inside were empty, but there were a few people at the bar, and the same bartender was there in the same greyish white apron. I walked up to the bar and ordered a drink. The bartender gave me a hard look but said nothing. I gave him a dollar for a forty-cent whiskey and told him to keep the change. Then I said:

"It was a terrible thing that happened to Mrs. Land last night."

63

"Yeah." His round black face set sullenly.

"How did she act before she left here? Did she show any signs of depression?"

"She was feeling lousy. She was dead drunk."

"There wasn't anybody with her?"

"Look, mister," he said in a grudging whine. "I had the cops sitting in my lap this morning. I told them what I knew. There wasn't anybody with her. How about letting me forget it?" He began to scrub the pock-marked surface of the bar with a wet rag. He scrubbed furiously, as if he were expunging all traces of the memory of Bessie Land.

The front door opened and let in a gust of winter which swept the length of the room. The bartender looked over my head. There was a look in his eyes, a glazed look of surprise and warning, which made me turn. A tall thin Negro in a tan overcoat and tan fedora paused at the door, caught my eye, turned and went out.

I ran the length of the room and went out after him. It was the Negro who had warned Bessie Land not to talk. When I got to the street he was already at the corner, walking swiftly with his head thrust forward and his coat-collar turned up. He looked back over his shoulder, and I caught a glimpse of his lean harried face in the glare of the corner streetlight. He began to run, and I ran after him, my feet sliding on the packed snow.

I began to gain on him. He looked back and saw that I was closer. I increased my pace, coming down hard on my heels to keep my footing. Two-thirds of the way down the long block there was a building with a boarded front. He made for it, went up the snow-piled steps in two bounds, and disappeared through a narrow plank door in the boarding. I followed him as fast as I could. Once he got away into the warrens of the tenements I'd never catch him.

The plank door opened on a blackness so solid it was almost tangible, and an inhuman silence. I closed the door behind me. Probably he was crouched in the hall waiting for me, and I didn't want to be outlined against the light from the street. Inside the building there was still no sound.

I took a cautious step forward, feeling for the floor with the toe of my shoe. There was no floor to find. I lost my balance and fell into empty blackness. After what seemed a long fall, during which I held my breath and all my muscles became rigid, I landed on all fours with a crash. Before its echoes faded, a door opened and closed above and behind me. The man I had been chasing had baited an elephant trap for me, waited inside the door for me to fall into it, and gotten away.

It felt as if I had landed on a rubbish heap. I searched with my hands and found some wire, a couple of tin cans, handfuls of what felt like dust. Then I remembered my lighter and lit it. A fat grey rat bustled out of the circle of light, his naked tail dragging behind him. I was standing up to my ankles in ashes, in a jungle of twisted pipes, charred timbers and shapeless wreckage. I understood gradually that I was in the basement of a tenement whose interior had been destroyed by fire.

I took a letter out of my pocket and set fire to it. By its light I found a blackened concrete stairway in the corner, and made my way out of the pit. I edged along the narrow ledge of the foundation to the door. There was something about the empty shell of the burnt-out building which made me shiver, like a core of desolation in the heart of the city. Even the streets of dirty snow were human and cheerful in comparison.

In the street, there was no sign of the man I had been chasing. I realized the impossibility of finding him in the black city. I had no idea of his name and only a vague impression of his appearance, and the people of his own race would hide him from me. Still, I had to try. I brushed off my trousers and overcoat as well as I could, and went back to the Paris Bar and Grill. It seemed a long way.

The bartender looked at me this time with hostility that was almost open. "I poured out your drink. I thought you wasn't coming back."

"I don't care about the drink. Who was that man in the tan overcoat?"

"What man in the tan overcoat?" he said with elaborate puzzlement. "I didn't see no man in no tan overcoat."

"Yes you did. The man that came in just before I left. The man that ran away when he saw me."

"Oh, him. Did he run away? I thought he just came in and didn't like the looks of the place so he went away again."

"He was here last night."

"Oh no, not him. Never saw him before in my life."

"He was sitting beside Bessie Land," I said.

His face had gradually become an idiot mask. "I guess you know better than me, mister. Never saw him before in my life. Another drink?"

I restrained my impulse to call him a liar, and walked out. Obviously I was getting nowhere on my own. I needed professional help. I walked quick with anger, three blocks before I caught a taxi. I told the driver to take me to the Federal Building on Lafayette Street.

It was past office hours, but there was still a girl on duty on the floor occupied by the Federal Bureau of Investigation. I told her that subversive activities were on my mind. She ushered me into a bare, well-lighted office which contained a polished walnut desk and four chairs. A minute later a heavy-set red-haired young man in a grey business suit came in, shook hands, and said:

"My name's Hefler. Ensign Drake? Very glad to know you. I believe you want to lay an information, as they said in the eighteenth century."

"Information is what I'd like to have."

"Be glad to help in any way I can." He darted a sharp look through his soft smooth voice. "We're very strong on cooperation with the armed services. You've probably heard of some of our activities in Hawaii?"

"I should have had sense enough to go to you in Honolulu. This second death might have been avoided."

He had begun to lean on the desk, but the word "death" straightened his thick body. "You'd better sit down, Mr. Drake, and tell me what you know."

I told him the things, from Sue Sholto's death to the man in the tan overcoat, which seemed to have a bearing on the case. He took shorthand notes in pencil on a memo pad. When I had finished, he went on writing for several minutes. Then he said in the tone of a lecturer:

"There are several leading questions to be answered, Mr. Drake. I realize that you can't answer them. Maybe we can. One, is Black Israel a criminal and/or a subversive organization? Mrs. Land's death suggests that it may be criminal. Hector Land's announcement that he intended to desert after joining Black Israel suggests that it may be subversive. We will investigate Black Israel."

"I went to Dr. Wanless in Ann Arbor today, but he didn't know much about it. He advised me to try an intelligent Negro."

"I see. Question two is closely connected with the preceding. What were and are the activities of Hector Land? Where did his money come from, and why did he run away? Did he kill Sue Sholto? Did he kill his wife, Bessie Land?"

"He was in San Diego three days ago."

"He could be here now," Hefler said impatiently. "We'll trace him. The third question is so inextricably bound up with the others that if we answer them we can answer it. Assuming that they were killed, why were Miss Shoto and Mrs. Land killed? You've advanced a conjecture of your own, Mr. Drake, and I'll be candid enough to say, strictly off the record, that I'm inclined to agree with you."

"I've suggested several possibilities," I said. Hunger, unbroken strain and the bright glare of the ceiling light combined to make me feel dizzy. "Which exactly do you mean?"

"In our present uninformed state," he went on in his dry abstract language, "we won't pin ourselves down to anything more specific than a generalization. It does, however, appear likely that the two women were killed because they knew too much, whether guiltily or innocently, about some subversive or enemy-inspired activity. Perhaps it involved suborning members of the armed forces. Perhaps it included collecting information for Tokyo. In any case, it is our task to find out. One of the first things we'll do is see about picking up your man in the tan overcoat."

"It's a relief to feel that I'm not in this by myself."

"I'm grateful to you for coming to us, and I hope we'll be able to keep in touch with you as the matter progresses."

I got up and started to move towards the door. The bright clean office high above the city, and Hefler's wordy talk, made the whole affair seem unreal. I wanted to get away into the dark. "I'll be in town for the next ten days. I'd like to call you in a day or two, and see if you've answered any of those questions."

"Call here and ask for me by name. Hefler. I don't need to tell a naval officer that this matter is confidential."

"Naturally. Good night."

A remarkably smooth customer, I thought, as I rode down in the elevator. If there were any more bodies to be discovered, I hoped that Mr. Hefler would discover them. At any rate, the affair was out of my hands. Or such, at the time, was my illusion.

It was nearly nine o'clock by my wristwatch. Mary would be expecting to hear from me. I called her hotel from a pay phone in the postoffice and she answered her room phone on the first ring, "Sam?" There was impatience in her voice.

"I'm sorry for calling so late. I had some business to attend to." If I could avoid it, I didn't intend to tell her about Bessie Land's death.

But she knew. "I saw the papers, Sam. It frightens me."

"It frightens me, too. That's why I—" I broke off. Hefler had said the case was confidential. I supposed that included Mary, though she knew almost as much about it as I did.

"Why you what?"

"That's one of the reasons I want to see you tonight. I need cheering up."

"I do, too. But I've got some good news to tell you. News isn't always bad."

"I'll be over right away. Have you had dinner?"

"Not yet. Give me twenty minutes to dress."

"Not a minute longer."

68

"You're sweet." She hung up, and I rushed back to the apartment to change my clothes.

She came to dinner in a dark-blue knitted evening gown which made her shoulders dazzling. Her yellow hair was upswept from her sleek neck like a bright summer flower on a graceful stalk. The sight of her changed my mood. She symbolized all the bright soft pleasant things which I had been missing for a year. Beside her young beauty, warm and glowing across the candle-lit table, the dark things which had happened in the night outside seemed impossibly ugly and fantastic. For a time they seemed the shadow violence of fiction, the falseface evil, the wax-dummy death.

Over our Martinis she asked me about Bessie Land's death. But Bessie Land had receded into another country.

"God knows what happened. I don't. Anyway, it's out of my hands."

"What do you mean?"

"The police are handling it. It's their business, and they think it's suicide, so as far as I'm concerned it's suicide." The Martini went through my empty stomach into my veins and made me say: "I came on this leave to have some fun, and I'm going to have it if half the population of Detroit falls dead in their tracks."

She looked at me with a cold half-smile. "You're pretty callous, aren't you, Sam?"

"Most people are. I'm just being candid about it."

"I suppose you're right. Most people are too busy looking out for number one to care much about anyone else." She finished her cocktail and lowered her glass. She looked at me with the air of one who has swallowed a hard truth and been strengthened by it.

"Of course the callousness isn't entirely real," I said. "Puncture the outer crust and you'll find a weak gruel made out of sour grapes, spilt milk, and wounded feelings."

"Block that metaphor. Are you really such a cynic as you pretend to be?"

"I don't know. I've been in the Navy so long I don't know what I'm like. But I know what I like. You."

69

Her eyes, half-transparent and of indeterminate color in the candlelight, looked narrowly into mine. "I can't make you out. I can't make out whether you're an intellectual or a roughneck."

"Both," I said lightly, but I was secretly flattered by the discussion. "I'm an intellectual among roughnecks and a roughneck among intellectuals."

"Whatever that means. What do you care about?"

"I used to think I wanted to be a great reporter. You know, to put my finger on the shame of the cities and all such stuff. But that petered out the last year or two."

"Isn't there anything you want? And if you say me I'll scream."

"I'm pretty sure I want to make money, I don't much care how. That's happened to more than half the men I know in the Navy. Get badly frightened a few times and you lose your idealism."

Her lips parted and her eyes were inwardly intent on something that she was going to say. Just then the waiter arrived with some dishes. She didn't say it.

We ate in silence for a minute or two. Then she said: "We won't be seeing much more of each other."

"I know. Two more weeks."

"Two more days. I've been offered a job in San Diego. That's my news."

"I thought you said it was good news."

"It is. It's a pretty good job. In the Naval Supply Depot."

I didn't like the prospect of her going away, and that made me captious. "It'll probably fold when the war ends."

"I know. But while it lasts I'll feel I'm—you know, making a direct contribution." She flushed slightly, and her voice was embarrassed. "I went into the whole thing with the Navy today, and it's settled."

All I could think of to say was: "I wish I was going with you."

"Why don't you?" Her smile was challenging.

"Maybe I will. You say you're leaving in two days?"

"If I can get a reservation. I have a priority."

"Anyway, I'll come and see you in Diego before I go out again."

"Why don't you come with me on Saturday? We could have a wonderful trip." Her clear eyes, reflecting the flickering candles as tiny moving flames, held the promise of a warm soft-lit room.

That night as I lay by myself in my bachelor bed, I thought of what a wonderful trip we could have. After all, there was nothing to keep me in Detroit. My girl had married and gone away. Most of my friends were in uniform and on other continents. And the one person I really liked to be with was going to San Diego and wanted me to come along.

I went to sleep without making up my mind, but in the morning it was made up for me. I was awakened by the telephone beside my bed.

"Ensign Drake?"

"Speaking."

"This is Hefler. We just got a teletype I thought you'd be interested in. Keep it to yourself, of course."

Hangover and sleepiness made my voice a little sharp. "There aren't more than one or two spies in the room." Joe Scott was huddled in his blankets in the other bed, sleeping like a dead man.

"You understand we must take precautions," Hefler said in a school-teacher's tone. "I called to tell you that we've gotten word on the whereabouts of Hector Land."

"Is he in Detroit?"

"Far from it. A big Negro answering to his description crossed the Mexican border at Tia Juana three days ago. He used a stolen Identity Card and a stolen Liberty Pass. As of this morning he hasn't re-crossed the border. A search is being made for him."

"I appreciate your calling, Mr. Hefler."

"I thought it might put your mind at rest to know that Land is nowhere near Detroit. Good morning." He hung up.

Joe rolled over in bed and sat up with a grunt. The early morning greyness of his face was stippled with black beard. "Who the hell makes phone calls this early in the morning?" he said.

"A friend of mine."

"I didn't know Hefler was a friend of yours. That was the name I heard, wasn't it?"

"Yeah, but keep it to yourself. He asked me not to talk about it."

"Is he after this Hector Land?"

"I said I wasn't supposed to talk about it."

"O.K., O.K., we won't talk about it." He yawned elaborately, giving me a view of the fillings in his wisdom teeth. "It's just that I came across something last night that I thought might interest you. The paper put me on the background of the Land case. Only now I can't tell you about it on account of we took an oath not to talk about it, didn't we?"

I threw a pillow at his head. He caught it and threw it back.

"Spill it," I said. "And don't tell me I can read it in the papers."

"You can't read it in the papers," Joe said more seriously. "It's not that kind of a story. The city editor killed it but quick."

I lit a bitter early morning cigarette, tossed him the pack, and waited.

"If Land deserted from the Navy," Joe said, "he had some reason for it. I'm not saying he had justification, but he had what may have looked like a reason to him. The boy had a raw deal, there's no getting around that."

"What kind of a raw deal?"

"I'm telling you. Hector Land's brother got killed in the '43 riots. Somebody slugged him with a club and smashed his skull. Hector was with him when it happened, and he went hog-wild. He tore into a streetful of whites and started to throw them against the walls of the buildings. It took a squad of police and a straitjacket to quiet him down. But that's just half of it. Do you know what the cops did then?"

"Jailed him."

"That's right. On a charge of aggravated assault. For beating up a couple of thugs that maybe killed his brother, he gets three months in the clink waiting for trial. He walks out of the clink into the Navy. That's not a hell of a good background for making a black boy all eager and excited to fight a war for democracy and equal justice. Or is it?"

"It doesn't excuse him for doing whatever he's done." I had to add: "But it helps to explain him. Is that the straight dope?"

"Straight out of the court records."

"Hefler will want to know about it, if he doesn't already."

"There's something else you can tell him," Joe said in his monotonous grating voice. "When Hector went to jail his wife got fired from her job and started hustling to make a living for herself. She's been hustling off and on ever since, until the last few months. A few months ago she suddenly got prosperous, and quit."

"How do you know that?"

"From Kate Morgan. Mrs. Land's ex-roommate."

"Did Kate Morgan know where she got the money?"

"Mrs. Land said she got it from her husband. She didn't say where *he* got it." Joe's mind skipped to another matter then, but I could follow his train of thought: "Could Wanless tell you anything about Black Israel?"

"Not a thing. Except that he didn't know anything about it, and nobody else seemed to, either. They avoid publicity."

"That's suspicious in itself," he said. "Your ordinary above-board Negro club or society is only too glad to get a little publicity. I asked Kate Morgan about it, but she wouldn't talk. Maybe she didn't know anything. I don't know. It's more likely she was scared. She saw what happened to Bessie Land."

"Do you think Black Israel killed Bessie Land?"

"How the hell should I know? Anyway, it's Hefler's baby now." He yawned again and retreated into his blankets.

73

I called Hefler back, and told him what Joe had told me. Then I got up and dressed. It was Hefler's baby all right, but I couldn't drop it. I had already made up my mind to go to San Diego with Mary. San Diego is a half hour's drive from Tia Juana.

PART III

TRANSCONTINENTAL

6

Two days later, on Saturday morning, Mary and I left Chicago on the Grand Canyon Limited. The best we could get on such short notice, even with a certain amount of priority, were parlor-car seats from Chicago to Kansas City, and berths from Kansas City on. When we boarded the train in the Chicago station we found that our parlor-car reservations entitled us to two seats in the club car.

The train was not due to leave for half an hour, but the club car was crowded. The air was hot and heavy with the undesired physical intimacy of wartime train journeys. People occupied their seats in attitudes of defiance, as if daring you to displace them. Mary and I found our seats, which were unoccupied, and sat down to wait for Kansas City and the semi-privacy of a compartment ten hours away.

The uneasy postures of everyone in the car, the atmosphere of suspended tension as if life had stopped and wouldn't start again till the train moved, the shabby upholstery and worn carpet, reminded me of an unsuccessful dentist's waiting-room. I said to Mary:

"In a minute a nurse is going to poke her head in the door and tell us that Dr. Snell is ready for the next patient."

She smiled a little fixedly without turning her head.

I tried again: "I've often wondered why so many people go away on a train for their honeymoon. They know they'll have neither comfort nor privacy. The honeymoon is one of the three or four most critical periods in life, but away they go to spend it in a box on wheels."

"At least we're not on a honeymoon," she said. "I don't see anybody else that is, either."

She went on studying the other passengers, temporarily more interested in them than in my attempts at conversation. Our seats were at the rear end of the car, next to the bar. That was strategic. Across from us was a middle-aged woman in a grey fur coat which might have been chinchilla but probably wasn't. There was a girl beside her, eighteen if she was a day, dark and pretty and bright-looking. Every man in the car had already paid her the tribute of a once-over followed by another once-over.

The girl's eyes were soft and dark, but they weren't shy. She was returning the once-overs. "Don't stare, dear," said the woman in the almost chinchilla coat. Evidently the relationship was that of mother and daughter.

My first impression had been that the mother was comfortably middle-aged and content to be out of the running. When she took off her coat I had my doubts. She wore a dress ten years too young for her, her bosom was carefully disciplined and exalted, and her waist was corseted to the point of exquisite extinction. The sort of woman, I thought, who is eager to be mistaken for her daughter's older sister and never is. I found out later that her name was Mrs. Tessinger and her daughter's name was Rita.

Rita's interest in her fellow mortals refused to be slapped down. She was watching with the innocent arrogance of the late female teens a man of thirty or so who was sprawled in a seat on my side halfway down the car.

His face was long and sulky, blue-black where it had just been shaved. His eyes were small and black, set close together as if in competition. From his parsimonious temples receded a stiff brush of hair as black and coarse as the tail of a black horse. He wore a blue serge suit with an air of having been born in one. He made me think of a brunette Uriah Heep. It took me a long time to learn his name, but when I did I never forgot it.

"I wonder what he's grousing about," Rita Tessinger said, as if he were ungrateful for the privilege of breathing the same air which she breathed with such pleasant undulations of her diaphragm.

"Don't make personal comments, dear," said Mrs. Tessinger, like a record prepared by Emily Post.

78

"What other kind of comments are there?"

"We could talk about the weather," the woman on the other side of Rita said in tones of husky amusement. "Hellish, isn't it? Those lake winds shrivel the flesh on my bones. Me for the sunny South."

"I love the South," said Rita, to indicate that she'd been there. "But I love Chicago too. It's so exhilarating."

"It's a big city, that's one thing you can say for it. But I can get fed up with a big city."

She spoke as if she had seen a good many big cities. I wondered in what capacity. She was a sharp-nosed woman in her fifties with an overpainted weatherbeaten face, but with something of an air which even her taste in clothes couldn't completely destroy. She wore a wool suit of robin's egg blue, and a flame-colored blouse which matched the color of her highly decorated cheeks. Beneath the mascara camouflage her eyes were old, bland and shrewd. When her hands moved, a small travelling museum of junk jewelry clinked on her arms. Her hands moved constantly, shaking in a steady tremor of senile ecstasy. Yet she had an air. She looked like a woman who had been through a great deal and come out with money, or with power in some other form.

Mary caught me watching her and, with the impersonal cattiness of women, whispered: "Isn't that hat a fright?"

It was. It was large and haphazardly plumed. The whole woman was a fright. But the man next to her didn't seem to think so. He looked sideways at her frequently with naïve interest.

At first glance, his interest in such a woman was the most noticeable thing about him. His plump, uncertain joviality, his carefully cut and thinning hair, his healthy shoulders becoming infiltrated by fat, his thick silk ankles crossed in front of him, his severely pressed and already crumpling grey pin-stripe suit, and his expensive and passionate tie announced: I am a successful American business man. His hands were large and hard-looking, indicating that he had once worked with them. He wore a handsome ruby ring, indicating that he would never work with them again.

The train trembled and came to life, jerked two or three times and began to move, and the successful American business man took his cue.

"It's great to get under way, isn't it?" he said to the object of his interest. "I thought we were never going to get going."

"Me either," she replied. "California here I come."

"You live in California, do you?"

"More or less. Mostly more. Do you?"

"No, I can't say I do. I have business interests there, take me down there two or three times a year. But I've never been able to stay long enough to get sick of it."

"What business are you in?"

"Well, I have investments in various types of enterprise. Oil, for one thing. As a matter of fact, oil is getting to interest me more and more."

He talked about the oil business.

Without a man to talk to, Rita estimated me, was challenged by Mary's glance, dropped her eyes demurely, soon became restless again. She tapped a small neat foot on the rug, and puffs of dust rose up like smoke from little distant explosions.

"Don't fidget," said Mrs. Tessinger, without raising her fine eyes from *Mademoiselle*.

The morning wore on, and no one appeared to man the bar. The suburbs of Chicago fled backwards into merciful oblivion. The quick, monotonous rhythm of the train's movement worked into my consciousness and beat there like a tiny extra heart. I began to get the feel of travelling, the slow excitement of escape.

After Bessie Land's death every Detroit scene had a thin margin of nightmare, every Detroit building had a sub-basement of horror. I had told myself that I was going south to look for Hector Land, but I knew I was also running away from a city which had turned ugly in my eyes, and a problem that had become too tough.

One thing alleviated my feeling that I was evading responsibility, the fact that the FBI was working on the case. Hefler had attended the inquest on Friday, and had told me enough to assure me that it wouldn't end there.

He already had investigators at work on Black Israel, and while they were gathering their facts it was just as well to let Bessie Land remain officially a suicide.

I tried to convince my conscience that I had done and was doing what I could. Still, my sense of relief told me that I was running away. But it was soon borne in upon me that my running was as effectual as that of a squirrel in a wheel or a whippet on an endless oval. Wherever I went the rats had tunnelled under the streets. I thought I was taking a trip for the hell of it, but I found out that I was being taken for a long ride.

The first call for lunch brought me out of my thoughts.

"I haven't been a very brilliant companion recently," I said to Mary.

"So what? I like you when you don't talk, maybe even better."

"I want to be loved for my eloquence alone."

"No man ever was. Come on, we'd better get in line before it gets too long."

Standing in line behind her I blew on the back of her neck and said: "Anyway, the things I want to say to you couldn't be said with people looking on."

She responded with the least pressure of her shoulder against my chest. The morning, which had seemed rather dismal, became a success, and the thought of the fun we were going to have on the trip went to my head like wine. The hangover from a wine jag is the worst there is.

An old lady directly in front of Mary turned around to look at her and, finding her appearance sympathetic, said:

"Isn't this an outrage, making us stand in line for lunch like this? I declare, if I had known it was going to be like this, I'd never have left Grand Rapids!"

"There are a lot of troops moving these days," Mary said.

"Well, you would think the government would make some arrangement for people that pay their way." The old lady noticed my uniform and became silent. Mary looked back at me with a quick smile.

"It used to be a real pleasure to eat on a diner," the man behind me said. "Now I eat what I can get and call myself lucky. After all, there's a war on. Isn't that right, sir?"

It was the fat man in the oil business. I turned to acknowledge the question and saw that the woman in the flame-colored blouse was with him. Perhaps he was a faster worker than he looked.

The line slowly moved up to the diner, and we ended up at a table for four, with Mary and me on one side, and the oil man and his companion on the other.

"My name's Anderson," he said, reaching across the table to constrict my hand. "I'm very pleased to meet you, Ensign."

"Drake is the name. This is Miss Thompson."

"And this is Miss Green," Anderson said.

Miss Green displayed teeth which were a little too good to be true, and said in a light bantering way: "So you two aren't on your honeymoon, after all. The way you looked at each other I thought maybe you were on your honeymoon."

Mary blushed and said, "We're just friends."

"Oh, well, you're young yet," Miss Green said surprisingly. "You've got plenty of time."

"It's us older folk that have to gather us rosebuds while we may," Anderson said. "Isn't that right?"

Miss Green laughed without meaning and lit a carmine-tipped cigarette with an automatic lighter. The tremor of her hand made the flame flicker steadily like a candle in a light draft. Something intangible about her reminded me of hospitals, and I wondered if she had a serious disease.

"I suppose you're on leave, eh, Mr. Drake?" Anderson said. "I envy you young men the experiences you're having in this man's war."

"Yes. I was in the South Pacific for a year." I looked at him more closely. He wasn't so old. In his middle forties, perhaps. But it was hard to tell about a face like that, plump and pleasant with unintelligently boyish blue eyes.

"That's one of the things I like about a train journey," Miss Green said. "You're always meeting new people, and I never get tired of meeting new people."

"Neither do I," Mary said, with a shade of irony in her

tone. "Trains, ships, street-cars and buses are great places for meeting new people."

"Also funicular railways and houseboats," I said.

Miss Green wasn't so dull as she'd seemed at first. She let out a laugh which ended in a fit of coughing. Between gasps she said, "Don't forget the subway."

"One of the finest things about America is the way Americans make friends so easily," Mr. Anderson said. "Some of the most interesting contacts I ever made are people I met on trains, people I never saw before and will never see again. How about that, Mr. Drake?"

"Yes," I said.

We had a mediocre lunch enlivened by a good deal of such conversation. When we made our way back to the club car Mr. Anderson and Miss Green were still with us. He seemed to have taken a liking to me, and I learned with a sinking heart that he was going all the way to Los Angeles.

He made up for his conversation, however, by announcing that he possessed a bottle of Scotch. He proposed to break it out in order to cement our transcontinental friendship. From a creaking new rawhide bag he produced a quart of Teacher's Highland Cream. The steward had appeared in the bar and gave us setups, and we had a round of highballs.

"Now this is something like," said Mr. Anderson. "How about it?"

I told him that this was something like.

Mr. Anderson said a few well-chosen words on the immense future of the oil business.

The man next to him leaned forward with his elbow on his knee in a respectfully listening attitude, as if he had been waiting for a long time for a chance to hear about the future of the oil business, and this was it. He was a sandy-haired little man with the ambiguous face of a clown or a character-actor. His features contradicted each other. A bold forehead and a timid chin, the coarse battered saddlenose of a pug and a delicate emotional mouth. His eyes were blue and completely empty, ready to contain anything.

83

They seemed especially ready to contain Rita Tessinger, who was the real reason for his leaning forward. He hadn't caught her eye yet, but he would. Every now and then he permitted his gaze to wander from Rita to the bottle of Scotch, which Anderson had set down beside his chair.

On the second round Anderson offered him a highball. He drank it quickly and expressionlessly, uttering a soft sigh when it was gone.

"You're a pal," he said. "I've got some bourbon in my suitcase but it can't compare with this. Nothing can. My name's Trask, by the way, Teddy Trask. Call me Teddy, everybody does, and it's only fitting. I was named after Theodore Roosevelt. My father was a Bull Moose Republican, still is. He hasn't voted since 1912."

There were introductions, and before long another round of drinks.

"Funny thing," said Teddy Trask, speaking loudly enough to be heard by Rita Tessinger. "I was over in Scotland not so long ago, and couldn't get any Scotch for love or money. I come back to the States and what do I get? Some Scotch."

"What were you doing in Scotland?" Mary said.

"Mr. Anderson," said Teddy Trask. "You're a unique man. You are the man who gave me the first drink of Scotch I've seen in six months. Nowhere in Europe could I find a drop of it."

Rita Tessinger was watching him with bright interest. Mrs. Tessinger raised her eyes from her magazine, sniffed inaudibly, and returned to her reading.

"Excuse me," Teddy Trask said to Mary. "I was in Europe entertaining the troops. Three shows a day for six months. Some fun. Now they want me in the Pacific. Where's Trask? Nimitz says to MacArthur. We want Trask. So here I go."

"What sort of a show do you do?"

He took a cigarette out of Anderson's left ear and lit it with a bewildered smile. Rita Tessinger laughed excitedly.

"I'm a magician," Teddy Trask said. "I'm an illusionist. I also read minds."

Rita spoke for the first time. "Please do some mind-reading. I'd love to have my mind read."

"Anybody but yours. I like you the way you are, mysterious." She blushed at the outrageous compliment, but swallowed it whole.

"Anyway, I do wish you'd do some more tricks. I think tricks of magic are utterly fascinating, don't you, Mother?"

"Utterly," said Mrs. Tessinger flatly.

But Teddy Trask needed no urging. He opened a black leather suitcase and made his preparations. Then, for an hour or more, he showed us his bag of tricks. He changed a glassful of rice into a whiskey highball. He performed all the variations of the ring trick. He did things with cards and found unexpected objects in Anderson's breast pocket, in Miss Green's hat, in Rita Tessinger's purse. The train crawled across the flat snowbound farmlands of Illinois, crossed the frozen Mississippi, and began to crawl into Missouri. The bottle of Scotch became empty and Teddy Trask and I opened our bottles of bourbon.

Mrs. Tessinger broke down and had a highball, and allowed Rita a short one.

"You said you could read minds, Mr. Trask," Rita said when he was packing up his gear. "I think it would be awfully interesting if you'd read somebody's mind."

"I shouldn't have shot off my mouth. I can't do much in that line without a helper."

"I'll help. Just tell me what to do."

He grinned like a satyr. "I'd like to take you up. But I need a trained partner. Right now my partner's in Frisco."

"Is she going out to the Pacific with you?"

"It's a he. Unfortunately. Sure he is."

"I don't understand why you need a partner."

"Well, you can do a one-man mind-reading act, but that takes preparation. It's much better as a two-man act. Joe and I have a pretty tricky little routine. You should see it sometime."

"I'd love to."

He poured another round of highballs and passed them

around. "A very tricky little routine," he insisted amiably over his fresh glass. "I usually stay on the stage and Joe goes down in the audience. So he asks a guy to take something out of his pocket or a woman to take something out of her purse and hold it in their hand. Right away—I'm up on the stage, see?—I tell the audience what it is. Now how do you think I do that?"

"I suppose you have some sort of a system of signals," I said.

"This certainly is interesting," said Anderson, with a boyish pleased smile.

Everyone at our end of the car was listening, except the dark man with the long sullen face. He was half-turned in his seat, frowning out the window at the water-ravaged earth of northeastern Missouri as if he felt personally responsible for it.

"Sure, we have signals," Teddy Trask went on. "We've got a dozen systems. For example, Joe touches his left eye—it's a lipstick. He touches his right eye—it's a watch. He smooths his hair—it's a handkerchief. That's the simplest kind. But say I'm blindfolded, that system doesn't work. I'm blindfolded, can't see a thing. What do we do then?"

"You could have verbal signals," I said. "Key words that would mean something to you, but not to anybody else."

"Say, this boy's sharp. Isn't this boy sharp?" he said to Anderson.

"Sharp is absolutely the right word for him," said Anderson.

"Sure, we use key words," Teddy went on. "But you'd never figure our best system. Our best system is a honey. Get this. Joe and I practiced counting together with a metronome. We set it for one beat per second and practiced counting with it, must have been three or four hours a day for a month. We got so we could count together up to a hundred and always be both on the same number.

"O.K., we're putting on a show. I'm up on the stage, blindfolded. Joe's down in the audience, talking. He gives me the signal to start counting, and we both start

86

counting together. He goes on with his line of patter, talking and counting at the same time. Then he gives me the signal to stop. We both stop counting, and we're both on the same number, see? Let's say it's thirty-five. Thirty-five is a lady's brooch. Forty-five is an automatic pencil. Every number has a meaning."

"That's wonderfully clever," Rita said. "But what if it's something you haven't got a number for?"

"That's practically impossible," Teddy said proudly. "There only are a hundred things that people carry in their pockets or their purses. Of course we have to change some of the meanings for a military audience. But not as many as you'd think."

"I thought I knew a little about codes," I said. "But this is the first time I ever heard of a time code. Did you invent it?"

"Sure. Joe and I invented plenty of them. I tried to tell the Army Signal Corps about some of them, but they weren't having any. They seem to think all they're good for is entertainment."

I noticed that the small black eyes of the man by the window were watching him. His impassive ophidian stare made me feel vaguely uncomfortable. He was as silent as a snake, and his long heavy-shouldered body had some of a snake's quiet menace. I was interested in Teddy Trask's codes and wanted to hear more about them. They struck my mind with a sense of unexplained excitement, like an answer to a question which had troubled me once but had been forgotten. But I decided to wait for a time when we'd have more privacy.

I met Teddy in the smoking compartment a few minutes later, and thanked him for the entertainment.

"Always glad to oblige," he said with a wide rubbery smile. "Keeps me in practice. By the way, what do you think of that Tessinger girl?"

"She's as pretty as hell. If I didn't have other irons in the fire—"

"Yeah, you have, haven't you? That girl of yours is as slick a blonde as I've seen for a long time. You've got your hands full, but not everybody can have his hands full of that kind of a package."

"You seem to be doing all right with Rita."

"Sure I am. And I like 'em young. I'm getting so I like 'em so young they look as if when you touch 'em they'll smear. It looks as if I'll have to break down the old lady first, though. But that shouldn't be so hard."

"Have you got a system for that, too?"

"Watch me," Teddy said. "Just watch me."

7

UNDER the influence of the pleasant tedium of motion, the fading effect of whiskey, the soft advance of night, I felt comfortable and sleepy and a little sad. While I sat holding hands with Mary, the train became a luminous worm boring through a continent of darkness. Our lighted car was a center of life and brightness moving in a mysterious shadow pinpointed by the infrequent lights of lonely farms and lost static towns.

She yawned charmingly, curled in her chair like a kitten, and brushed my shoulder with her cheek. "A penny for your thoughts," she whispered.

"I was thinking about Teddy Trask's code."

"Damn you, I thought maybe you were thinking about me. Give me back my penny. I might as well be holding hands with a mechanical thinking machine."

"You put your penny in the slot, and that's what came out. I'm not responsible for the workings of my fine well-oiled brain."

"Well-oiled is the word. Well-oiled with whiskey. And what was the thinking-machine thinking about Teddy Trask's code?"

"I was thinking that a code like that might possibly be used by an enemy agent. Remember the argument I had with Eric that day in Honolulu? All the codes and ciphers I knew about involve the use of letters, numbers or words. But a code like that of Trask's could be used without any of them. A monitor wouldn't even know he was listening in on a code."

"I don't get it. But you go right ahead and think about your codes, and I'll think about all the interesting men I've met in my life."

"Have I been neglecting you?" I squeezed her hand.

"You're not now. Maybe I won't think about all those interesting men. As a matter of fact they weren't so *very* interesting."

At dinner we sat with an army officer named Wright who had boarded the train at Fort Madison. He was a short rotund man about forty, wearing the oakleaf of a major and the insignia of the Army Medical Corps. His interest in Mary was too obvious and self-assured to please me. His special field was the psychiatry of battle exhaustion, and he gave us a lecture on it with the air of a peacock spreading his tail-feathers.

In the diner I noticed that Teddy Trask had contrived to share a table with the Tessingers, and that Mrs. Tessinger was beginning to regard him with some favor. Anderson and Miss Green, at a table by themselves, seemed to have found a great deal to talk about.

Shortly after eight o'clock we reached Kansas City, where our Pullman was to be added to the train. There was a half-hour wait, and Mary and I, along with most of the other occupants of the club car, left the train for a breath of air and a walk on the station platform. When our time was nearly up, an army private carrying a large canvas bag came up to me and said:

"Can you tell me where Car 173 is, mate?"

"Isn't that our car?" Mary said. "It'll probably be down at the far end."

The three of us walked down the platform and found Car 173, which was the last car on the train. I left Mary in our compartment and went back to the club car to fetch our bags. When I got back to the Pullman most of our friends from the club car were there: Major Wright, Anderson and Miss Green, the Tessingers with Teddy Trask hovering helpfully about them. The old lady from Grand Rapids had one of the two drawing rooms to herself, and I noticed some time later that the dark man with the sulky face had the other.

The soldier who had asked me his way was sitting in our compartment with Mary while his berth was being made up. He was a young-old man somewhere between 25

90

and 35, with a lean tanned face and a long lanky body. He said his name was Hatcher. He wore the European Theatre ribbon with three battle stars, and the bottoms of his khaki trousers were tucked into high field boots. I noticed when I sat down beside him that he was a little drunk. I myself was feeling no pain.

As the train began to move he said in a soft voice that had probably originated as a Missouri drawl: "Well, I wonder when I'll get to see K.C. again."

"Home on leave?" I said.

"Brother, you said it. And what a leave. Wowy. I've seen London and Paris and Shanghai, but K.C. is the town for me. I spent seven hundred and forty dollars in two weeks, and it was worth every cent of it."

"You didn't see Shanghai in this war."

"This war has been going on longer than some people think. I was in Shanghai in '37. I was a seaman on a British freighter. After that I had a berth on a British passenger ship in the Yangtze fleet."

"You should be in the Navy."

"I tried to get into the Navy, but I couldn't pass the physical. I was in good enough physical shape to move in on Sicily and walk across Normandy, but not good enough to get into the Navy. What do you know about that?"

"I've always said the infantry had it tougher than anybody else. The Navy has a pretty quiet time, unless your ship gets hit and you have to swim for it."

"This is the most unusual Army-Navy debate I've ever heard," Mary said with a smile.

"Well, it's the truth," I said with somewhat alcoholic emphasis. "I know damn well the chief reason I applied for a commission in the Navy was so I wouldn't be drafted as a private in the Army."

"Say, brother, I like your attitude," Private Hatcher said. "You're open-minded, even if you are an officer. How about a drink on it?"

He started to get up but I stopped him. "I've got a bottle right here. Half a bottle anyway."

We each had a drink but Mary turned it down because we had no mixer.

91

"You say you spent some time in China in the thirties," I said. "Did you see anything of the Chinese war?"

"I saw the rape of Nanking. It's something I won't forget." His gaze turned inward, and his face lost its cheerful expression. Mary looked at him with interest, but said nothing.

With something compulsive in his voice, something reminiscent of the Ancient Mariner, Hatcher went on: "The ship I was on was hauling passengers out of Nanking up the river to Hankow. Most of them were European, British and French and Russian and some Americans, getting out of Nanking while the getting was good. This was in the winter of 1937. We loaded up the ship for the last run—we didn't know it was going to be the last run but it was—but we couldn't get any food for the passengers. We lay off Nanking fully loaded with passengers for a day and a night, while the first mate beat out his brains trying to get something for them to eat. There was food in Nanking all right, see, but the Japs had moved in on it.

"On the second day the first mate went into town, and took along me and five other fellows who knew how to shoot. We were supposed to be a sort of bodyguard. I'll never forget that walk along the wall to the city. I've seen things in Europe since, but nothing like that. On both sides of the wall for it must have been a couple of miles, there were piles of corpses, stiff and starved-looking and sort of thrown together and tangled in heaps. It's the only time I ever saw human beings treated worse than cordwood."

Mary was pale and her eyes were large and bright. Hatcher noticed this and said: "Excuse me. I shouldn't be shooting off my mouth like this. Anyway, you can see why I'm sort of looking forward to getting into the Pacific half of the war. I never felt just the same way about the Germans, but I reckon that's because I never saw a Nazi concentration camp."

"Did you manage to get food for your passengers?"

"Yeah, we got in touch with a black market operator. He was a white man, too, can you beat that? But he had an in with the Nips all right. I guess he'd cornered just about all the rice in the city, and he was asking monopoly prices. The first mate finally got about fifty bags, but it didn't do much good."

"Why not?"

"When we were one day up the river the Nips bombed the ship. Nearly everybody got off her, but she burned right down to the water. We had a hell of a time getting back to Shanghai. After that I got out of China." He smiled slightly. "I thought I was getting out of China for good, but I bet I'm there a year from now. I'd like to meet the little yellow-belly that dropped that bomb."

Anderson moved past us down the aisle. I offered him a drink, and he joined us. I told Mary that I'd go to the club car and try to get some setups, but Anderson said:

"I don't think he'll sell you any. Kansas is a dry state."

"I've had enough to drink anyway," Mary said.

I hadn't. We continued to work on my diminishing bottle. Anderson had a short one and went back to Miss Green. The porter started to make up our berths, and Mary went to sit with the Tessingers while Hatcher and I moved down to the men's smoking-room.

He leaned towards me and said in an elaborate alcoholic whisper: "Is that fat guy a friend of yours?"

"No, I just met him on the train today."

"What's his name?"

"Anderson. He's in the oil business."

"So his name's Anderson, eh? And he's in the oil business, eh?"

"Do you know him?"

"I don't know," he said slowly. "I reckon maybe I do. *If* I do, it's going to be very interesting."

"What do you mean?"

"Oh," he said, "he just looks like an interesting kind of guy. I've always been interested in the oil business."

If I had been in another mood his evasion would have made me curious, and I'd have tried to cross-question him. But the pulse of good whiskey was beating in my body like a long lifting swell. I was swathed in the mellow calm of semi-drunkenness. At the distance of the day's journey and the Olympian height from which I regarded them, even the deaths of Sue Sholto and Bessie Land seemed unimportant. Their ruined bodies were trivial things, broken dolls remembered from somebody's childhood. The whole dark world outside the train window was unreal to me. The only reality was the bright moving room in which I sat drinking with an interesting companion, and the reflection of my own stupidly complacent face in the dark pane.

Hatcher had taken a crumpled envelope from the breast pocket of his khaki shirt, and was fumbling in his other pockets.

"What are you looking for?" I said. "Name it and you shall have it."

"I've got a letter here I've got to get off. I'm damned if I know what happened to my pen."

I handed him mine. He told two folded sheets from the crumpled envelope and spread them out so that I could see that they were closely covered with handwriting. Holding a magazine on his knee he began to write on the back of the second sheet, moving his lips as he silently spelled out the words to himself. If I had been a lip-reader I'd have known the contents of his postscript, and perhaps been able to save his life.

When he had finished he replaced the amplified letter in the envelope and gave me back my pen. I noticed that the letter was already stamped and addressed, and marked 'Airmail.'

"I should have got this off before. Girl-friend," he said. "Do you know if there's a place I can post a letter on the train, or do I have to get off and post it in a station?"

"There's a mailbox in the club car. It's a glass box on the wall between the writing table and the bar."

"Thanks." He sealed the envelope and went away. But he reappeared in the doorway in a few minutes carrying a bottle of whiskey. The letter was still in his other hand.

"Your whiskey's all gone," he said. "Try some of mine."

He handed me the bottle and went away again. The label on it, which was unfamiliar to me, announced that it contained Rare Old Bonded Kentucky Bourbon, Aged Five Years, Ninety Proof. I broke the seal and uncorked it with

94

the corkscrew on my penknife. I thought I detected the rough rank odor of fusel oil, but I suppressed my doubts and poured myself some in a paper cup. It wasn't a smooth drink but it was warming, and at that stage I didn't care.

Hatcher came back, having posted his letter in the club car, and asked me how I liked his liquor.

"It's terrible," I said. "But I've drunk worse."

His first drink made him snort. "It's terrible all right. With this liquor shortage, I had to take what I could get, but the guy that sold it to me said it was real bonded stuff. God knows I paid enough for it."

"I wish I'd brought more liquor from Chicago," I said. "I forgot about these dry states. Say, maybe Anderson has some more. I'll ask him."

Anderson was sitting with Miss Green in a darkened compartment at the other end of the car. Close together, with their faces turned to each other, they looked incongruously like lovers. But what they were talking about, from the few words I caught before they noticed me, was the oil business in New Mexico. It occurred to me that perhaps he was trying to persuade her to invest money in one of his enterprises.

I broke in on their oleaginous endearments and told Anderson how liquorless I was. But he said:

"I'm sorry, old boy, but you and your friend will have to drink what you've got or go dry."

"He's your friend too," I said.

"What do you mean by that? I never saw him before in my life."

"Maybe he's seen you somewhere. He was talking as if he knew you."

There was a trace of impatience in Anderson's voice now. "Well, I'm afraid I can't help you anyway. That Teacher's was all I had."

I underwent one of the swift changes of mood which occur in an alcoholic state, and became suddenly ashamed of myself.

"Excuse me," I said to Anderson, and bowed low to Miss Green. "Excuse me for disturbing you so tactlessly."

"Hell, that's all right, old boy," Anderson said heartily. "It happens to all of us. I'm only sorry I can't help you out."

Mary left the Tessingers, who were on the point of going to bed, and joined me in the aisle. Most of the berths were made up now, and the car had shrunk to a high narrow tunnel between green curtains. Some of the unreality of the world outside had seeped into the train. For a moment I had a sense of terror, as if the dim aisle were an ancient path in an unknown jungle where dangerous creatures waited in ambush.

"We're coming into Topeka," Mary said. "Let's go out on the platform and have a look."

We made our way to the platform at the rear of the car. Topeka was a scattering of lights, a series of warehouse walls broken by glimpses of almost deserted streets stretching drearily into darkness, then a quickly extinguished vista of neon lights grinning in many colors on the unheeding heads of after-movie crowds, finally the long irregularly lit platform of the station. One of a hundred such cities that one saw for the first time with remembering boredom, and left immediately with relief. My jag was running down like an unfuelled engine, and I felt very sorry for all Topekans, whose city was a poor gathering of feeble lights in the immense darkness of the hemisphere.

Mary slipped her warm hand between my arm and my side. "When I was a little kid I was very poor," she said dreamily. "I used to watch the passenger trains come into the station. It was the bottom of the depression, but there were still plenty of rich people to ride them. I had never been on a train, and it seemed to me that the men and women behind the lighted windows were like kings and queens on thrones."

I was touched by what she said, but distrusted the sentimentality. "Every kid feels that way about riding on trains," I said. "But once you've taken a few trips the illusion collapses. The parts of cities you see from trains always seem to be on the wrong side of the tracks."

"I've still got my illusion. I feel more alive when I'm on

a train. It gives me a feeling of power to ride across the country and leave the rest of the world sitting."

"I guess you've never grown up. Maybe you're lucky."

"Maybe I am, but it's sort of painful. Now I'm the lady in the lighted window, but I still see myself the way I did when I was a kid. I'm on the inside looking out, but I'm on the outside looking in, too."

"You're schizophrenic," I said, and kissed her.

The baggage and mail had been loaded, the travellers taken aboard and the doors closed behind them. The brakemen swung their lanterns and the train began to move, laboring toward the staccato frenzy of speed.

Her mood changed suddenly, and she said:

"I shouldn't have spent so much time with the Tessingers, but I couldn't resist the situation. Mrs. Tessinger must know as well as I do that Teddy isn't interested in her, but she's a woman, and she just can't help being grateful for his flattery. He's been saying the most outrageous things, and she eats them up."

"Such as?"

"Oh, everything. Her beauty, her youthful spirit, her energy, her clothes. Tomorrow, I expect, he'll go into all the anatomical details."

"What's Rita's reaction?"

"Admiration, so far as I can see. She knows what he's doing, and she seems to be all for it. She's spent the last few years in a very conservative girls' school."

I took hold of Mary and kissed her again, hard.

"You *are* a little drunk, aren't you?" she said.

"Do you mind?"

"No, I'm very tolerant." She put her hand on the back of my neck, drew my head down, and kissed me. "Let's go in now, shall we? I'm cold."

We turned toward the door but before my hand found the knob, the door opened and Hatcher's long lean face appeared in the opening:

"Say, mate, I was looking for you. I been all the way up to the club car looking for you. How's about another drink?"

"Go ahead if you like it," Mary said. "I'm going to bed."

She kissed me lightly on the cheek and disappeared down the passageway.

"She's a sweet number," Hatcher said. "How did you happen to get in so close with such a sweet number?"

"I met her in Honolulu at a party. Then I met her again in Detroit."

"Some guys are born lucky. She looks like warm stuff to me."

"Even if I am not entirely a gentleman," I said with a certain pomposity, "Miss Thompson is a lady."

"Don't let her kid you. They all have the same instincts. The same beautiful instincts."

"Shut up, God damn it! I'm thinking of marrying this girl."

"Sorry. Sorry. You got your angle and I got mine. Play it the way you like it. How about that drink?"

"Anderson didn't have any. We'll have to drink yours."

"O.K., I was weaned on moonshine. Come on, I left the bottle in the smoking-room. Hope it's still there."

It was under the seat where he had left it. He fished it out and took a long pull from the mouth. I poured a little in a paper cup and drank it, but the interruption had spoilt my taste for drinking. Besides, the stuff was even more nauseous than I remembered. My stomach flopped over like a dying fish.

"Jesus," I said, "this stuff is terrible. Worse than any jungle juice I ever had."

"Oh, it's not so bad." In a spirit of bravado, Hatcher tipped up the bottle and took another long gulp. In the next few minutes he swallowed his adam's apple more frequently than was normal, but he managed to control any other symptoms of queasiness.

He sat back and lit a cigarette and told me some of the things he had seen as a merchant seaman. The sailor in Canton who had his belly slashed by a razor and came running down the street with his bowels exposed. "Yeah, I heard they sewed him up and he got over it." Once on a little tramp steamer on which he shipped out of Australia he had a mad captain who slept every night with a lifesize rubber woman. Her painted rubber face, the captain's steward said, gradually grew paler from his kisses.

As he told that story, Hatcher's own face gradually grew paler. His bright blue eyes became glaucous and rolled slowly in their sockets. His speech became blurred as if someone had swaddled his tongue in cotton batting. " 'Scuse me," he said finally. "Don't feel s'good."

With his jaw hanging beneath pale parted lips he got up with an effort and lumbered through the door to the men's toilet. For a few minutes I could faintly hear the sounds of retching, like heavy paper tearing.

I didn't feel so good myself. The smoking room rocked cumbrously like the cabin of a ship riding a long deep swell. The lights in the ceiling divided like amoebas and danced like elves. I raised my right hand to my face in order to cover one eye and stop their insane reproductive dancing, but my fingers struck me across the bridge of the nose. I discovered that my hands were exceedingly remote objects, only partially animate and only nominally under my control. My whole body was growing numb, as if my nervous system were a live wire gradually going dead as the battery ran down.

It seemed to me that the train was slowing but perhaps, I thought, it was only my metabolism. Suddenly the train stopped with a jerk, lights outside the window became as fixed as my eyes could hold them, and my stomach flopped over again like a dead fish turning in its grave.

Hatcher was still in the men's room, so there was only one thing for it: I had to get outside. On legs which were as hard to handle as rubber stilts I got out into the passageway. The walls seemed to expand and contract on either side as I edged my way between them across the buckling floor to the door.

I stumbled out onto the open platform into cool night air under a high clear sky. The stars descended upon me like an elevator in a shaft.

8

As THE falling stars entered the narrow field of my consciousness they patterned themselves in circular groups which began to turn. Rotating towards each other the wheels of stars clustered like grapes into a turning silver fist, a rolling white eyeball, a seed of light which eloigned itself in darkness until it was a remote chink in a bellowing heavy curtain and finally swallowed up. Then the low sallow sky of unconsciousness, starless as the skies of hell and roiled and weaving at the desolate horizon with dusky orange smoke, blossomed suddenly in an intricate array of turning wheels. In time with a low humming which rose and fell like the sourceless ululation of cicadas, the wheels spun monstrously in geometric patterns.

My surviving speck of consciousness was as helpless and hurried among them as a grain of sand caught up in the churning of a millwheel. Yet the innumerable millwheels churned an element as intimate as my blood.

Come as close to death as you may, there is no complete cessation of consciousness. The mind's torment clings to the flesh till the heart has stopped and the brain dies. While I lay straddled by nightmare my mind, lost in the horrible interior of my body's engines, prodded them into continued effort. My diaphragm wrestled with paralysis and won. I went on breathing.

The dark wheels lost their motion and their shape, extending, like a spattered gout of blood, blood-red fingers which groped among the unknown terrors of my situation. I lay in a jungle of dark weaving tendrils and limp leaves which swayed and bowed like sinuous feathers in a desultory wind. When I opened my eyes this soft inconstant world was resolved into the real world of solid dimensions.

But a trace of the movement persisted in a teetering of the whole universe above me. The fulcrum of this motion was the small of my back, which seemed ready to break under the strain.

I was conscious of a dark rectilinear shape, as fearfully palpable as the lid of a tomb, which loomed between me and the night sky. Reflected dimly by this huge and shadowy object, I saw faint lights, some fixed as stars, one or two moving like comets in remote orbits. Like a voice calling across stellar space, I heard a faint "All aboard!" A light moved in an arc near me. I became conscious, in a blinding flash of terror and recognition, that the painful fulcrum on which my back rested was a rail. I was under the train and it was about to move across my body.

Simultaneously I let out a yell which was drowned in the snort of rushing steam, and flung myself forward. I struck my head on a brake rod. Grovelling and scuttling like a lamed crab I dragged myself out from under the wheels and flung myself on the platform beside the rails.

"What the hell!" somebody said.

I turned on my back and sat up, and a brakeman came towards me swinging a lantern.

"Hold the train," I said in a hoarse voice hard to recognize as my own. "I'm supposed to be on it."

He moved his lantern in a signal and I lost my feeling that the train was pawing the ground with its steel hooves. "Look here," he said. "What were you doing under the train?"

Self-pity and the hammering and droning in my head made me bark irritably, "Lying there. For fun."

He took hold of my arm and dragged me up: "You get up on your feet and give me a straight answer. This train can't wait all night."

My legs were still only partly under my control, but I balanced myself on them.

"What's the matter, you sick?" the brakeman said. "Say, you're drunk." He shook me by the shoulder. I struck his hand away.

The conductor came up, biting impatiently at his heavy grey moustache. "What's the holdup here?"

"I was unconscious," I said, unnerved into childishness because I had never been unconscious before. "Somebody put me under the train."

"He's drunk," the brakeman said. "You can smell his breath. He says he's on the train."

"Well, get the hell back on or I'll call the Shore Patrol. Wait a minute, let me see your ticket."

"It's in my berth. Don't you know me?"

The brakeman raised his electric lantern to the level of my face and the conductor gave me a narrow-eyed look. "Yeah, I know you. Climb back on and get in your berth. You're lookin' bad, boy. And if you make any more trouble this trip, any trouble at all, the S.P. will put you off the train."

There was no use in arguing and I was uncertain of my grounds anyway. I transported my roaring head and raw throat down the platform to the end of the car, up the iron steps, in the door, down the passageway toward the men's smoking-room. Before I got there the train had begun to move. Remembering my flashing terror of the wheels, I had a swelling sense of relief, like a man walking on a grave in which his own empty coffin has been buried.

My relief gave way to blank wonder and then to another terror when I saw that the men's smoking-room was empty, and found by experiment that the door of the men's room was locked. I knocked on the door. There was no answer. I knocked more loudly, until the sound of my knocking echoed in my tender skull like the blows of a metalsmith's hammer. There was still no answer.

I tried the knob again and rattled the door in its frame. Then it occurred to me with a pang of shame that I was acting like a child. Hatcher, of course, was in some other part of the train, probably in bed by this time.

But the door was locked, and it locked only on the inside. If there was anyone in that little room capable of speech, he would have answered. "Hatcher!" I called through the wooden panels. "Hatcher!"

"What's the trouble?" someone said behind me. "Gotta go bad?" I turned and saw Teddy Trask wearing a purple

102

silk bathrobe over candy-striped pajamas, and carrying a shaving kit.

"I think there's a sick man in there. The soldier that got on at Kansas City."

"My God, you don't look so good yourself. Where'd you get the dirt all over your uniform? Let me see this door."

He tried the knob and examined the narrow space between the door and its frame. "We'll soon find out." From his shaving kit he took a new safety razor blade, unwrapped it deftly, and applied it to the crack of the door.

When he had been hunched over his work for perhaps a minute I heard him say "There!" and the bolt snapped back in its socket. He turned the knob and opened the door, but it wouldn't open far.

He forced it a few inches more till the space was wide enough for his head, and looked around the edge of the door.

"My God!" he said. "What's the name of that Army doctor down the line?"

"Major Wright."

"I'll go and get him."

He hustled away, his slippers lapping the floor in quick syncopated rhythm. I took my look into the little room.

Hatcher was kneeling on the floor in a posture similar to the Moslem attitude of prayer. Most of the weight of his body was supported by his legs, which were bent under him. His head, turned sideways, rested on the edge of the toilet bowl. The wall light two feet above his face allowed me to see that his one visible eye was staring blankly at the blank wall. There was about him a souring sweet smell of sickness and drugs.

I tried to get in to him, pressing my shoulder against the door, and he moved suddenly. He fell sideways into immediate stillness like a loosely filled sack. I felt such pity for his helplessness and indignity, which I myself had so nearly matched a few minutes before, that I cried out.

"Here, here," Major Wright said behind me, taking

hold of my shoulder with one hand. "Let me see what I can do for him."

While I stood back on unsteady legs and watched, Teddy Trask, who was smaller than I, stepped around the door. He maneuvered Hatcher into a more nearly upright position, embraced his chest from behind, and brought him out into the smoking-room where he gently laid him out on the floor. Hatcher's face grinned bleakly at the ceiling.

The doctor made a quick examination, attempting to take his pulse, inspecting his chest and mouth for signs of breathing. When he touched a staring eyeball with his finger I winced and turned away, but not before I had noticed the absence of any reflex. Private Hatcher's eyeballs were as insensate as glass.

"I'm afraid he's dead," Major Wright said, squinting at me over his shoulder through rimless spectacles. "What made him sick?" There were marks of Hatcher's sickness on his rumpled uniform.

"We were drinking some pretty terrible liquor," I said with shame. "I passed out, too."

"It would take a good deal of liquor to kill a man like that. How much did he have?"

"I don't know. Maybe a pint in the last couple of hours."

"Is there any of it left? I want a look at the stuff."

The bottle of Bonded Bourbon was in plain sight on the floor near Hatcher's limply spread field boots. At the sight of it my nerves crawled. I picked it up with aversion and handed it to him. He uncorked the bottle and took one sniff. His squinting little eyes narrowed to two steel edges.

"This man's been drinking ether," he said. "No wonder he's dead."

He recorked the bottle quickly and replaced it on the floor.

"Those poor bloody dog-faces never learn," Teddy Trask said. "Two of my buddies in France drank poison liquor. One of them died, and the other's blind."

Major Wright looked at him sharply at the word 'dog-faces.' He said to me: "How much of this stuff did you drink, Mr. Drake?"

104

"A couple of short ones. But that was enough to put me out. How long did we stop at that last place?"

"Emporia? About five minutes. Why?"

I told him why.

"Do you suggest that someone deliberately dragged you under the wheels of the train?"

"I don't suggest it. I state it. I know I didn't do an Anna Karenina under my own power. I passed out on the rear platform, and if I'd fallen from there I'd have fallen either behind the train or to one side. I couldn't have fallen under the wheels."

"You can't tell what you did when you were unconscious. Ether makes people do some awfully funny things."

"Such as die," I said.

"That's true too. All the ether addicts eventually die if they keep it up. Where did this bottle come from?"

"He bought it somewhere in Kansas City. I think someone poisoned it."

"Someone on the train, you mean?"

"Yes."

"We'd better get the conductor and the Military Police," Major Wright said.

"I'll get them." Teddy Trask slapped away again.

"That's a genuine seal on the bottle, isn't it?" I said.

He examined it near-sightedly. "Looks like it to me."

"I broke that seal myself. I even smelled it when I opened it. It didn't smell so good, but I didn't smell any ether."

"You didn't smell the ether when you drank it, either. Some people don't have a very good sense of smell, especially when they've been drinking. I think your olfactory evidence is questionable."

I admitted sheepishly that that was true.

"Smell this." He uncorked the bottle and passed it quickly under my nose. "Do you smell ether?"

"I can't be sure. I'm not very familiar with drugs."

The odor was a pungent, sweet and nauseous mixture. It reminded me of hospitals and of something else which I couldn't place.

105

"That's ether all right," he said. "I'd stake all the money I ever earned in anaesthetist's fees on it."

"Is ether ever used in cheap liquor to hop it up?"

"I've never heard of it. But you can't tell what these bootleggers will do. I'd never touch bootleg alky myself."

A combination of things, the sick hospital odor in the air, the dead man on the unswept floor, and my own reaction from fear, made me dizzy again. The room lost weight and reality, became a foul shape-changing bubble in a dark stream. For a minute I held on to the curtain in the doorway with both hands. Then by an effort of will I focussed my eyes and mind again. But I felt shaky.

Major Wright was watching me narrowly. "See here, you're looking terrible. Sit down on this seat."

He took my pulse and listened to my chest. "You couldn't have got a great deal of that stuff, or you wouldn't be up and around. An ounce taken internally is enough to kill a man. But you've got to remember ether poisoning sometimes has secondary consequences. You go to bed now and let me look at you again tomorrow."

There was the sound of several footsteps approaching in the passageway. "I'll go in a minute. But first I want to talk to the conductor. That's probably him now."

The conductor came in preceded by his paunch and followed by a Shore Patrol man. He was biting his moustache hard as if the tobacco which stained its fringes was edible but bitter.

Then he saw the dead man waiting on the floor. A tremor of nervous anger went through him, from his knees through his belly and heavy shoulders to his multiple chin.

"What in God's name happened?" he said.

Major Wright took natural charge of the situation. "This man is dead. I'd say it was ether poisoning, though I can't be sure without an autopsy. The dead man and Ensign Drake here were drinking poison liquor."

The conductor raked me with a hard old eye. "That's what you were doing under the train, eh? Don't you know it's illegal to drink liquor on a train in the State of Kansas?"

"It's more illegal to poison people," I said unpleasantly. "Somebody poisoned that bottle."

He picked up the bottle and examined it, turning it over and over in his hands. His palms were netted with dark lines like a railway map.

"Where did the liquor come from?" the S.P. man said. He added a perfunctory "sir."

Wright answered him. "Private Hatcher—the man there on the floor—got it in Kansas City. The stuff's got ether in it."

"Look here," the conductor said suddenly. "This is how the ether got in."

He had turned the bottle up, and the discolored nail of his right forefinger pointed to something in the bottom. It was a small circular flaw in the center of the thick round glass.

"I've seen this done before," he said, "mostly during Prohibition. In my state it would be technical homicide."

"What is it?" Major Wright said.

"Somebody who handled this liquor drilled a hole in the bottom of the bottle and extracted the good liquor. Then he refilled the bottle with his own deadly concoction, and sealed the hole with molten glass."

The S.P. man, who was young and eager, said: "I've seen that done, too. You can change the liquor without opening the bottle and breaking the seal. It's a quick way to make money. If you don't care what happens to the people that drink the cheap stuff."

"Murder is a quick way to make money," the conductor said solemnly. "This is technical homicide."

"What do you mean?" I said.

"The salesman who sells poison liquor is legally responsible for its effects. That's probably the Missouri law the same as it is where I come from. But it's going to be an awful job finding the liquor store where this bottle came from."

My certainty that someone on the train had poisoned the bottle was dissolving and trickling away. I had a hard time trying to think clearly.

"Does this mean it couldn't have been poisoned on the train?"

"It sure looks like it," the S.P. man said. "You don't get equipment on a train for melting glass and drilling bottles. It's this consarned liquor shortage that does it. These fly-by-night sharks know that the boys will drink anything if it's all they can get, and they take advantage of it. We get more trouble from bad liquor than from everything else put together."

"Damn it!" I exploded. "I didn't walk under the train by myself."

Major Wright put his hand on my shoulder. The paternal effect was spoilt by the fact that he had to reach up. "You can't tell what you did. Maybe it just looked like a comfortable place to lie down."

The light dazzled me. My eyes were sore and heavy in my head. My throat felt raw, as if someone had reamed it out with a file. "This is the third death," I said. "Yet nobody seems to give a damn. Don't people get tired of all these deaths?"

The conductor and the S.P. man paid no attention to me. They were making plans to get Hatcher's body off the train.

"Look," Major Wright said. "I like my work, but one corpse on my hands is enough for one evening. For God's sake go to bed. That's an order in two senses, professional and military."

"All right," I said finally. "I'll talk to you tomorrow."

"Good night. Pleasant dreams."

On the way out I heard him tell the conductor that he thought he'd close Hatcher's eyes, because the sclera of the eyeball was drying and turning brown.

The ladder was standing ready at my upper berth. As I started up on shaky knees, I noticed that the light in Mary's lower berth was still on.

"Sam?" I saw her white hand fumbling between the heavy green curtains, and then her face. Washed shining for the night, with her bright hair done up on top of her head, she looked naïve and very young, like a nymph peering between green boughs.

I said, "Good night."

"Sam, what's the matter with your face? What's happened?"

"Be quiet. You'll wake everyone."

"I *won't* be quiet. I want you to tell me what's happened. You've got a bruise on your forehead, and you're covered with dirt. You've been fighting."

"No, I haven't. I'll tell you in the morning."

"Tell me now." She reached up and took light hold of my arm. The confused alarm on her face was so flattering that I almost laughed.

"If you insist. Move over."

I sat on the edge of her berth and, in a low voice which grew steadily hoarser, told her what had happened.

More than once she said, "You might have been killed."

The second time I answered, "Hatcher was. By God, I don't believe it was an accident. Maybe that poisoned bottle was intended for me."

"How could anyone know that you were going to drink out of it? And didn't you say a hole had been bored in the bottom and resealed? That couldn't have been done on the train."

"I don't know. I *do* know one thing. I'm not going to touch another drink until I get to the end of this trouble."

My mind's eye was struck by the sordidness of the scene which had seemed jolly enough at the time: Hatcher and me sprawled on the shabby leather seats of the smoking-room drinking ourselves to death or to the edge of it. A strong revulsion placed me for the first time in my life on the side of the Women's Christian Temperance Union.

The remembered scene was so vivid that I could see every detail of the room, the brown bottle on the floor, Hatcher's thin lips mumbling over his letter.

"I wonder if it's still on the train," I said to myself.

I must have spoken aloud because Mary said, "What?"

"Hatcher's letter. He wrote part of a letter while I was with him and went to mail it in the club car. Maybe it's still there."

"Do you think there could be anything in it bearing on his death?"

"It's possible. I'm going to the club car now, before that letter's taken off the train."

I leaned forward to get up but she laid a restraining hand on my arm. "No. I'll go. You look terrible, Sam."

"I admit my head's swimming. I think it's trying to swim the English Channel."

"Poor dear." She patted my arm. "Please go to bed, Sam."

"See if you can read the name and address on that letter through the sides of the box."

"I will."

I climbed the ladder to my berth. It seemed very high. I took off my coat. It was such an effort that I played with the idea of simply falling back and going to sleep as I was, without undressing. I heard the heavy rustle of Mary's curtains falling to behind her, and then the soft rapid sounds of her feet retreating in the direction of the club car.

Then I heard fainter sounds moving towards me, a mere susurrus of feet so faint that it was suspicious. I opened a narrow crack in my curtain and peered down. Moving swiftly and silently like a panther in the jungle path which I had imagined the aisle to be, a man glided beneath me in the direction Mary had gone. All I could see was the top of his head and his shoulders, but I knew him by their shape.

When the door at the end of the car had closed softly behind him I climbed down the ladder and followed him. My mind, inflamed by shock and fear, hated the beady-eyed man so much that I hoped wildly I would catch him in some overt act, and have an excuse to club him with my fists. He had looked like an animal stalking game. I felt like another.

But when I stood on the shaking windy platform at the end of the club car and saw him again through the window in the door, he was standing in the passageway quietly doing nothing. Rather, he was standing with his face turned away from me, intently watching the interior

110

of the car. Making no attempt to conceal my movements, I opened the door and walked towards him. He started and turned in a quick graceful movement and his right hand jumped unconsciously towards the left lapel of his coat. I deliberately jostled him as I passed him, and made contact with a hard object under his left breast which could have been a gun in a shoulder holster.

It was Mary he had been watching. She was sitting by the mailbox at the far end of the shadowy car, which was half full of sleeping people and dimly lit by a small light at each end. As I walked towards her among stretched-out legs, I tried to keep in the line of vision of the man in the passageway. She glanced up startled when she heard me. She had a pair of eyebrow pluckers in her right hand and Hatcher's letter in her left.

"Put it back," I said in a hoarse whisper. "You're being watched, and it's a Federal offense to tamper with a mailbox."

"You didn't tell me!"

"I told you to try to read the address through the glass. Now put it back."

There was so much intensity in my voice that her hand moved as if in reflex and dropped the envelope through the slot.

"Did you get the address?"

"No. It was your fault I didn't."

I looked back over my shoulder and saw no one in the passageway. "I didn't want you to get in trouble. There was a man watching you."

"Who?" The pupils of her eyes had expanded, making them seem almost black. Her mouth was soft and vulnerable, and her hands were trembling slightly.

"The black-haired man with the beady eyes. He was in this car this morning."

"Oh."

I crouched down and tried to read the address on the envelope, but it was lying in shadow. I lit my lighter and tried again. I couldn't make out the complete address but I saw enough for my purpose: Laura Eaton, Bath Street,

111

Santa Barbara. I wrote it in my address book while Mary looked on.

"Why are you doing that?"

"I'm going to go and see her. I want to know what's in that letter."

"Is it that important?"

"It's important. I'm getting very tired of people dying. People should die of old age."

Her hysteria suddenly matched mine. She rose with her blue silk robe sweeping about her in tragic folds and embraced me with arms so tense they almost hummed.

"Please drop it, Sam," she said. "I'm afraid you'll be killed."

"I'm beginning to think that's not so important. I don't like these ugly deaths."

"Don't you want to live, Sam?" Her eyelids held bright tears like evening dew on the closing petals of flowers. "Don't you love me?"

"I hate the cause of these deaths more. If you got off at the next stop I'd stay on. Perhaps you'd better."

Her mood changed suddenly. "Don't worry, I'll stay on. If you're going to be any good tomorrow you'd better get some sleep."

"You'd make a good wife." I kissed her.

"Do you think so, Sam? Do you really think so?"

A disturbed sleeper in the shadows behind us began to snore in loud protest.

"We'd better go to bed," I said.

We passed the dark man again in the vestibule of our Pullman. He was standing at the window looking out, but he turned and stared at us as we went through. Tension hung sharply in the air for a moment and the blood pounded angrily in my temples. But I could think of nothing to do except to go to bed.

When I closed my eyes in my berth, it swayed like a windswept treetop. Outside my cell the train whistle howled desolately, and the night rushed by like a dark wind. Where are we going? I wondered in languorous desolation, and then in sleep moved confusedly among blank staring eyes. I wandered among forests of dead flesh beside typhoid streams, and emerged in an open space where a hunch-backed spider cocked his beady eyes at me and scurried away on many legs. The sun was bloody red and throbbing in the lowering sky, a beating heart which as I watched it became pale and still, and the pulse of the world stopped. I wandered in the desert of the dead world, its rotting crust crumbling beneath my running feet till it gave way utterly and I fell endlessly in a soundless void.

The worried and impatient face of the Pullman porter appeared between my curtains and announced that it was noon.

9

I GOT to the diner on the last call for lunch. On the way I saw Mary in the club car, where she was talking with the Tessingers. She walked down to the end of the car with me. She looked fresh and untroubled, clear of last night's hysteria.

"Are you all right, Sam? You slept like a log all morning, and I hated to wake you."

"There's nothing I like better than sleeping in till noon. But it's the first time I ever had a hangover after twelve hours' sleep."

"You should stick to nice pure alcohol."

"I'm sticking to nice pure water."

"I know you are. Everybody's out of whiskey and we can't buy any from here on."

"It's just as bad as being at sea."

She leaned towards me and kissed me lightly on the cheek. "Is it?"

"Well, not exactly. Life was generally much more tranquil at sea, and much less interesting. There weren't enough women to go around—"

"None at all, in fact?"

"None at all, in fact. It's sort of nice having women around again. I've always wanted a dog, too."

"Dogs are easy to get."

"Not as easy as you think. I am a victim of a dog shortage. Behold me dogless."

"You *are* feeling better today."

"I had to. I couldn't have felt any worse."

"You'd better hurry if you want anything to eat. I had my lunch ages ago." She went back to the Tessingers.

The diner was still crowded, and my ears turned red as

I walked down the aisle between the alert tables. I knew what the old ladies of both sexes would be saying behind their hands. Practically drank himself to death. Think he'd have more self-respect. Gentleman by Act of Congress. Disgrace to the uniform he wears. The trouble was that the old ladies had half the truth on their side. In the white light of hangover, my actions of the night before looked criminally foolish.

Major Wright was at a table by himself and nodded to me to join him. "You're looking a bit better. Feeling all right?"

"Pretty good. My throat's still sore, though."

"Ether's a pretty powerful irritant. I'll have a look at your throat this afternoon."

Looking out the window I was struck, with the inextinguishable surprise of travelling, by the difference that a day's journey made. I had left Detroit and Chicago shivering in the grip of the northern lake winter. The prairie outside the window now was snowless and sunlit under a summer sky.

"Where are we? I haven't looked at the timetable."

"The Texas Panhandle. The last town we stopped at was Amarillo."

"The spring comes early up this way."

"It's the best time of the year here. It gets too hot in the summer."

The subject of the weather had been exhausted, and I asked him the question that was on my mind: "What happened to Hatcher?"

"His body was taken off at Wichita. I turned him and the whiskey bottle over to the Kansas state police. They're going to get the Missouri police to try and find the man that sold it to him. They seemed rather doubtful that they'll be able to. Kansas City is a big town."

"What will happen to his body?"

"It'll be shipped to his next of kin in Kansas City. He's got a brother there, according to his papers. They'll do an autopsy, of course. I would have liked to do that autopsy myself."

"I don't share your wish."

115

"It's a very interesting process. You retrieve the ether from the tissues by distillation. Gettler has described it, I believe."

Over our inadequate meatballs we watched the sere flat fields slide sideways past us. There was a charcoal smudge across the horizon from the carbon-burners in distant oil-fields.

"Hatcher's death has definitely been put down to accident, then?"

"I don't know what else you could call it, from his point of view, that is. From the point of view of the dealer, it's technical homicide."

"Isn't it possible that the bottle was poisoned on the train?"

"That hole couldn't have been made on the train."

"But perhaps the ether was added after I opened the bottle. It was sitting in there unguarded at various times."

"Who would be carrying ether on a train?"

"A doctor might," I said at random. "Are there any other doctors on the train?"

The suggestion didn't please Major Wright. His round face set in a frown of offended dignity. "I don't know, I'm sure. Members of the medical profession don't go around putting poison in liquor bottles."

"Of course not," I said soothingly. "You're satisfied in your own mind that Hatcher died by accident, then."

He didn't answer for a minute. Then he said: "From the physical point of view, yes. From the psychological point of view, it's not so simple. Hatcher must have known that he was drinking bad liquor. You did, too, didn't you?"

"I knew it was bad. I didn't know it was that bad."

"Still you must have known you were taking a chance. Then why did you drink it?"

"I wanted a drink, and that was the only drink available."

"Precisely. You wanted a drink. Why did you want a drink? Why did Hatcher want a drink? I'll tell you why. In a word, because life wasn't good enough for you. You wanted a little escape, a little death. Perhaps it was the war you wanted to get away from. Basically, though, you

116

wanted to get away from yourselves. Excessive drinking is deliberate suicide by degrees."

His discourse would have interested me at another time, but right now I had too many other things to think about. The night before I had intended to tell Major Wright the whole story. Now it seemed useless. His mind was made up, and it would probably be a waste of breath to try to change it. Even if I tried, what reason could I offer for Hatcher's death? And which of the passengers would make a plausible suspect?

I tried to go over in my mind the events which led up to Hatcher's death. My brief period of unconsciousness hung in front of the evening like a transparent curtain which distorted it. My memories of the night were empty glasses magically refilled, a warm ballooning sensation whirling towards the edge of nausea, snatches of conversation, too many cigarettes, sudden faces in the bright light. Anderson, Miss Green, the Tessingers, Teddy Trask, the dark man in the blue suit—I still didn't know his name, but Uriah would do. So far as I could recall, any one of them could have had access to the bottle. It had been unguarded in the smoker for at least ten minutes, while Mary and I went out on the platform to look at Topeka.

It seemed useless to try to eliminate people I knew. There were so many other people on the train whom I didn't know, and who might equally well have poisoned the bottle. Still, my mind had to take hold of something or it would tear itself to pieces like a motor with nothing to push.

Least likely first. The Tessingers. Rita was no suspect. She was a sweet kid only. A bobby-soxer in a bell-jar, waiting for somebody to lift the lid. Her mother, of course, was the lid. The old lady had some fire, especially since Teddy had been blowing on the coals. But the mind had to take a great leap to imagine her in a homicidal role. Mrs. Tessinger was something of a lady, a genteel woman if not a gentlewoman. She wouldn't permit herself to get mixed up in spying and murder, if only because they weren't respectable.

Major Wright. Sitting across the table from him and

117

looking at his face was enough. He was rather pompous and self-important, probably because he had short legs. But he was a good man.

Teddy Trask. He was an elusive character. Probably capable of a good deal of trickery, on and off the stage. But he just didn't seem built for murder. He had too much of a sense of humor, for one thing. For another, he had paid no attention at all to Private Hatcher. Besides, I liked Teddy.

Uriah with the short black hair. He puzzled me, and he made me angry. So far as I knew, he hadn't said a word to anyone on the train. Yet he was constantly popping up. I had a feeling that he listened to everything that was going on, and wrote it all down in a little black book. I made a resolution to see that imaginary little black book. And I hoped I had to fight him for it.

Miss Green. There was a good deal of experience in her face, not all of it acquired at strawberry socials and Sunday School picnics. I had seen brokendown dancers and aging party girls with the same desperate devotion to cosmetic youth as she had, and the same knowing old eyes. She looked like a woman who refused to be kidded. I wouldn't put crime past her, but it would have to pay. And it would have to be less risky than murder.

Mr. Anderson. A type which I had always disliked. My first impression was that he was a stupider and less interesting Babbitt. I still thought he was stupid, but he didn't fit so neatly into the Babbitt pattern. A woman like Miss Green was apparently his meat. He had a bluff silly jovial air, but he seemed to understand situations. The things he said gradually seemed to get less stupid, though they never got past average. Perhaps the main thing which made me distrust him was an impression of power he gave. Yet his whole approach belied it. The last thing a Babbitt will let you imagine is that he has a will of his own. Still I felt there was a raw low-grade power in Anderson. That wasn't much of a reason for suspecting him of murder, but I did.

Major Wright had excused himself and gone away, a little displeased by my lack of interest in his ideas. The

118

diner was empty of passengers, and the headwaiter was looking at me inquiringly. Something about the car, probably the Negro waiters in their white coats, reminded me of Honolulu House and Mrs. Merriwell.

It occurred to me with an unpleasant shock that perhaps my prejudices limited my thinking as much as her prejudices limited hers. After all, there was plenty of reason for thinking that Hector Land had killed Sue Sholto and run away to escape the consequences. And there was a Negro porter in our Pullman, a Negro I knew nothing about. For all I knew, he could be a member of Black Israel.

I found the porter sitting by himself at the end of our car. He was reading a magazine with such close attention that for a moment he didn't see me standing beside him. Then he looked up, closing the magazine on a black finger. It was the *Atlantic Monthly*.

Looking into his lined face, set in dignified reticence, I felt like a fool. I was about to question a man about a murder for the sole reason that he was black. Then something that Wanless had said to me came to my rescue. He had advised me to consult an intelligent Negro about Black Israel.

"Would you object to my asking you one or two questions?"

He stood up, leaving the magazine on the seat behind him. "No, suh. You can ask me any question. That's one of the things I'm here for, to answer questions."

"My question has nothing to do with your job, but it's important to me. Is there anywhere we can go to talk?"

"We can go to the vestibule, suh. There's nobody out there just now."

He followed me out to the vestibule, where the spring wind swept in through the open halves of the doors.

"My name's Drake," I said, and held out my hand.

He regarded it with cautious impassivity, as if it were a gift which might explode in his face. Then he took it perfunctorily, withdrawing his hand quickly as if from a trap. "Pleased to meet you, Mr. Drake, suh. Mah name's Edwards, suh."

He held his speech carefully in the Amos 'n' Andy tradition, the slurred speech which whites have learned to expect of Negroes and resent the absence of.

I realized that I was getting nowhere fast. "Look, Mr. Edwards"—I made the Mister as casual as I could—"I used to work for a newspaper in Detroit, and I've always tried to help your race. You'll have to take my word for that, but it's true. A few days ago a woman I knew, a Negro woman, was killed in Detroit. I have reason to believe that an organization called Black Israel had something to do with her death. I haven't been able to find out anything about Black Israel. Can you help me?"

"I don't mess with things like that, Mr. Drake. Except for our Brotherhood, I keep myself to myself."

"I went to Dr. Wanless at the University of Michigan. He advised me to consult an intelligent Negro."

"Professor Wanless? I heard him speak at a meeting in Chicago. He was a fine speaker." He had begun to use the plain Midwestern English which is natural to a Negro born in the Middle West and educated in the public schools. I felt that his resistance was lowering.

"I know that Black Israel is a Negro society. I suspect that it's the kind of thing that intelligent Negroes disapprove of. Can you tell me anything about its purposes and methods?"

"Excuse me, Mr. Drake, but what use are you going to make of anything you find out?"

"I'll tell you frankly I don't know. I do know that the FBI is investigating Black Israel. If I find out anything that they haven't already learned, I'll turn the information over to them. You see, I discovered the body of the woman who was killed. The night before she died I heard her mention Black Israel, and I heard a man, another Negro, warn her to keep quiet. I got the impression from what she said that Black Israel was subversive."

"So the FBI is after them," the black man said. "It's about time."

"You have heard of Black Israel, then?"

"I've been approached. But I'll tell you, Mr. Drake, I wouldn't touch Black Israel with a ten-foot pole. It started

120

out respectable enough but it went downhill fast. It's my own opinion that somebody got into it who had an axe to grind. At one time I thought it was the Nazis. That was in forty and forty-one, when Black Israel started to go rotten."

"The Nazis? What made you think that?"

"We had our own investigations, Mr. Drake. Investigations of certain—certain things which threatened to do harm to our cause. There was fascism behind some of the movements which claimed to speak for the Negro in America,—it was strong in Detroit. Our Brotherhood has always looked out for things like that."

"But you said you no longer think that the Nazis are behind Black Israel. What made you change your opinion?"

"The kind of propaganda they used, chiefly. You know the propaganda that some politicians put out whenever the Federal anti-poll-tax bill comes up on the floor of Congress. That the black race is inferior, unfit for political equality, closer to the apes, careless children for the white men to look after and teach to do a few simple chores?"

I suspected that, consciously or unconsciously, he was quoting from the editorials of the racist press, but his deep voice vibrated with sincerity. He knew what he was talking about, since he had lived intimately with it for forty years.

"I know the kind of stuff you mean. Surely Black Israel didn't use that sort of thing?"

"Oh, no, Mr. Drake. That's the point. Black Israel has the same line, but it's on the other side of the fence. They're just as violent for black supremacy as the Southern politicians are for white supremacy. Their line is that the day of the white races is over, and the colored races are coming into their own. It's a line that appeals to the unconscious desires of a good many people of my race, but all it can lead to is trouble. That's what the Nazis want, of course, but I can't imagine Hitlerites supporting propaganda for black supremacy."

"I don't know. Their motto is divide and rule, and they don't care how they do the dividing."

"But they've been backing the other corner. I know for a fact that there were fascist agents in some of the violent anti-Negro movements in Detroit. Dr. Wanless confirmed that in his talk on the race riots."

"They're quite capable of playing both ends against the middle. I'll admit, though, that the Black Israel propaganda you've described sounds more like the doctrine the Japs have been using in East Asia."

"That's exactly what I think, Mr. Drake. I've done some reading about the Japanese line in Burma, and this smells like a fish out of the same barrel."

"Do you know anything about the leaders of Black Israel?"

"They stay in the dark. Black Israel is a secret society. I've been approached—I told you that. I've listened to their come-on speech and I've read a couple of their pamphlets. That's all I know."

"Who approached you?"

He had been looking into my face as we talked, holding my attention with intent black eyes. Now he half-turned away and looked out of the open door. He ran the fingers of his right hand through his greying wool in a nervous gesture. Finally he said: "I won't tell you, Mr. Drake. And if you use the information I gave you, please don't mention my name."

"Black Israel is dangerous, isn't it?"

"You said that a woman you knew got killed."

"I won't mention your name. I'm very grateful for what you've told me. It was a pleasure to talk to you, Mr. Edwards."

"Thank you." A smile kindled on his lined and rather forbidding face. "Well, I better be getting back to work."

Before he went back into the sleeping car, a definite change took place in him. His large erect torso became somehow amorphous. Meaning went out of his eyes like a snake slipping into its hole. His movements became faintly shifty and apologetic, as if all his intentions were subject to change at a moment's notice on somebody else's whim. His personality shrank to fit the smooth black shell which white opinion has hopefully constructed for Negroes to live in. Watching this change, which I had never seen before because I had never before seen anything but the smooth shell, I felt a movement of anger and pity stir at the bottom of my mind. I felt that I had witnessed a partial death.

But the rest of my mind was vaguely elated. In less than three weeks I had stumbled across three bodies, each of which had seemed to be projected across my path violently and causelessly out of impenetrable darkness. Some of the shadowy horror of that darkness was beginning now to take form, becoming identifiable as a shape of human evil which I could begin to understand. Understanding it, I could fight it. I was determined to fight it. I hated the cause of those ugly deaths as intensely as I would have if Hatcher had been my brother, and the Jewish girl and the Negro woman my sisters.

Mary came to the door and joined me on the platform. "Mmm," she said. "I can smell spring in the air."

"Aren't you sick of eternal spring, after those months in Hawaii?"

"I was when I left, but a few days of northern winter made me homesick for spring again. Maybe I'll never go north again."

"Aren't your family in Cleveland?"

"Oh, yes. But they can come south. I really think that's what we'll do. What were you talking about with the porter?"

"I wrecked my blues last night. He's going to clean and press them for me."

"I like you in greys. It took you a long time to persuade him, didn't it?"

"Oh, we got to talking. I've always been interested in the Brotherhood of Sleeping Car Porters."

Later that day, when she would have less reason to connect my theory with my conversation with the porter, I brought up the subject of Sue Sholto's death.

"I don't believe Sue Sholto committed suicide," I said. "I made some inquiries in Detroit before we left, and I found out that Black Israel is a violent and subversive organization. I believe that Hector Land belonged to it,

123

and that his wife Bessie had learned a good deal about it, perhaps enough to put the finger on one or more of its leaders. Hector himself may be one of its leaders. In any case, I'm reasonably certain that Bessie Land was killed to keep her from talking. It's barely possible that she was frightened into killing herself, but if so, somebody connected with Black Israel frightened her."

"You started to say something about poor Sue," Mary said. She spoke as if the memory was painful to her, and I remembered the terrible jangling which Sue's death had given her nerves. "What has Bessie Land to do with Sue?"

"I'm becoming more and more convinced that they were killed for similar reasons, if not by the same person, by the same organization. Don't forget that Hector Land is associated with both killings, and he is definitely a Black Israelite."

"That's true," she said thoughtfully. "Perhaps he killed Sue after all. But why?"

"Certainly not for the reason Mrs. Merriwell gave. Her accusation was a red herring which really served to protect him by confusing the issue. Can't you think of a reason? I know you feel loyal to Sue's memory, but can't you think of anything which would connect her with Hector Land? You saw her every day."

"Sue lived a quite simple, ordinary life. She had love affairs, but you knew that. She wasn't promiscuous, she was monandrous while it lasted. Of course she was a Communist, but I don't see what that could have to do with it."

"She was a Communist?"

"Oh, I don't mean that she had a party card. Nothing like that, so far as I knew. She had Communistic views on some things, that's all. Perhaps I should have called her a fellow-traveller."

"What things?"

"Government ownership of heavy industry, the race question, things like that."

"She did, eh? Why on earth didn't you tell me that before?"

"I saw no point in bringing it out. It seemed irrelevant at the time. You know that the very mention of Communism to a great many people is like a red rag to a bull. It still seems irrelevant to me."

"It may be irrelevant, but I'm not going to drop it till I make sure. I'm going to ask the FBI to investigate Sue Sholto."

"Have you been to the FBI?"

"I didn't mean to tell you that. Yes, I have."

"Why don't you leave the case to them, then, Sam? Can't we forget it for a little while?"

"I know. We came on this trip together to have fun. I'm sorry it hasn't worked out that way so far."

"It never will," she said bitterly.

"Maybe I'm not as callous as I thought. I can't forget about the things that have happened. Or maybe it's just that last night they started to happen to me."

"Aren't you afraid?" Her wide stare searched my face.

"Yes. I'm afraid. But from now on I'm going to be more careful. Eventually I'm going to get my hands on somebody or something that I'll take great pleasure in choking to death."

"You make me shudder." She smiled palely, but her hand had involuntarily gone to her throat.

"Did I scare you? I'm sorry."

I looked around, decided that our compartment gave us enough privacy, and kissed her. Her head went down to my shoulder and her bright hair tickled my face. With my arms around her I could feel a light shiver run along her back. She leaned towards me and we held each other close. I breathed through her fragrant hair. I felt that she was more precious to me than a part of my own body.

She said: "Don't ever let me go."

"Excuse *me,*" Mrs. Tessinger said. She was standing in the aisle, smiling down at us with exaggerated tolerance.

We separated quickly, and Mary's hands went automatically to her hair. I started to light a cigarette, then remembered that smoking was forbidden in the Pullman.

"I didn't mean to butt in," Mrs. Tessinger said. "Would you two care to have dinner with us tonight?"

125

Mary looked at me and giggled. "Sam. There's lipstick on your mouth. Here, let me take it off."

She dabbed at my face with a handkerchief. I surreptitiously kissed her hand.

We had dinner with the Tessingers. Teddy Trask, who was inseparable from them by this time, made a fifth on a chair placed in the aisle. Mrs. Tessinger was extraordinarily vivacious. Her bosom seemed higher than ever, and her waist tighter. Rita sat by the window with an air of being left out of things. Every now and then she gave her mother a black glance edged with malice.

"I was so hoping you'd give us another performance this afternoon," Mrs. Tessinger said to Teddy. "Why did you let us down?"

"I didn't feel in the mood, after that nasty business last night. I guess not many other people did either." He looked pointedly at me.

"Do you really think you and that soldier were deliberately poisoned, Mr. Drake?"

"I don't know. The authorities don't seem to think so."

"I think Mr. Drake would rather talk about something else, Mother. The subject must be painful to him."

"The experience was painful," I said. "The subject isn't particularly. I'm afraid I can't be very entertaining on that topic, though."

"Teddy, do tell Mr. Drake and Miss Thompson those glorious shaggy-dog stories of yours. This man is priceless," Mrs. Tessinger said to us.

"But we've heard those stories, Mother."

"I'm sure that Miss Thompson and Mr. Drake haven't heard them. Even if they have, the way Teddy tells them, they're very well worth hearing again. Teddy, I insist."

With a deprecating smile, Teddy told a long and involved shaggy-dog story about a man who worked in a zoo and couldn't remember the names of the animals. Mrs. Tessinger kept up a low tittering. Rita looked out of the window. Mary watched the three of them with a faint smile on her lips.

He told the story well, but I couldn't keep my mind on it. Something kept prodding at my attention from below,

126

an unremembered fact in my unconscious which insisted on its importance and clamored to be remembered. When Anderson and Miss Green moved past us down the aisle, her junk jewelry tinkling like faint facetious sleighbells, I realized what it was.

Hatcher had said something about Anderson before he died, something which seemed to indicate that he knew him. The possible implications of this, strengthened, if anything, by Anderson's denial, hit me suddenly and hard.

Anderson had sat down a few tables away, with his broad impassive back to me. I felt like getting up and going to him then. But I stayed where I was, watching the plump whitish wrinkles in the back of his reddish neck, wondering what went on under that thin barbered hair, inside that stolid head.

Mary's hand found mine under the table. "What's the matter, Sam?" she said in a whisper.

"Nothing. I was just thinking."

"You've got a dreadfully one-track mind."

"I guess I have."

The story ceased, and we laughed dutifully, except for Rita. As if to convince herself of her own existence, she launched into a rapid strained monologue on all the things she was going to do in La Jolla, and what fun she was going to have. Mrs. Tessinger and Teddy exchanged long queer looks.

Then Teddy talked about his practically front-line experience in France. Mrs. Tessinger wreathed herself in girlish graces. Teddy seemed larger than he had the day before, as if somebody had blown air into him. I liked him better small.

Mary and I excused ourselves when we could, and made our way back to the Pullman. When Anderson came back with Miss Green, I went to him and told him I wanted to talk to him.

"Absolutely, old son," he said. "Any time. I hear you had some trouble on the train last night."

"Trouble is the word. Would you mind coming down to the smoking-room? There's nobody there just now."

"If you'll excuse me, Miss Green?"

127

"Oh, don't mind me. I've got a love-story magazine to read."

When we were seated in the smoking-room and Anderson had lit a cigar, I said: "Private Hatcher, the man who died last night, seemed to know you. Did you know him?"

"He must've made a mistake. I told you I never saw him before in my life." Anderson's smooth plump face was unruffled. His pale blue eyes were alert.

I said quickly on a hunch: "How did you get out of Shanghai?"

Preceding his statement by a pause of just the right length, he said with just the right combination of puzzlement and irritation: "But I've never been to Shanghai. What are you trying to get at?"

I was sitting on the leather seat beside Anderson, half-facing the door. There was no audible sound in the passageway, and no visible movement, but a subtle combination of sight and hearing made me conscious that someone was there. I got up and crossed to the door in one motion, and faced the dark man again.

I said in a voice that was ready to break with cumulative anger: "I'm getting bored with having a shadow. Get out of here."

His face was unmoved. He said softly: "Excuse me. I didn't realize that you were in a position of authority on this train."

"That has nothing to do with it. If I catch you eavesdropping again I'm going to slug you."

"If you slug me, as you so elegantly put it, I'll have you arrested. I may even slug you in return."

His black eyes were hard, steady and impenetrable. I felt an urgent need to surround them with matching black rings. But if I did, the Shore Patrol would put me off the train. My frustration was so strong and bitter that it gathered in a lump in my throat. I left him standing there and went back into the smoking-room.

"Let me give you a word of advice," said Anderson, who hadn't moved from his seat or shifted his cigar. "You're all keyed up, and I can't say I blame you. But if you keep on going around insulting people like this, you're

128

going to get into a peck of trouble. Just now you practically accused me of having something to do with that soldier's death. A minute later you accused that young man of eavesdropping. I know you had a tough time last night, but don't let it make a crank out of you."

The Dutch Uncle approach leaves me cold every time, and this was no exception. But I had no answer for Anderson except:

"I guess you're right."

"Better get some more rest," he said patronizingly as he got up to go. My impulse was to tackle him, throw him down and search his pockets for evidence of I didn't know what. I controlled my impulse.

10

SUSPENDED tensely between the desire to do something and unwillingness to make a fool of myself, I sat and smoked until the tension sagged and I felt able to sleep again. Then I called for the porter to make my berth. He came to the doorway and stood there regarding me grimly, his face like hewn basalt.

"What's the matter?" I said.

He moved nearer and said in sibilant disappointment: "Mr. Drake, you said you wouldn't tell anybody what I told you today."

"I haven't. But I didn't say I wouldn't. All I said was that I wouldn't identify my source."

"That's what I mean, suh. You said you wouldn't tell anybody that I knew anything about Black Israel." He glanced over his shoulder as if he feared that the cohorts of Black Israel might be massing outside the door to destroy him.

"I didn't and I won't."

"Maybe you didn't, suh," he said without belief. "But that man knows." He jerked his head towards the drawing-room.

"Who knows what?"

"Mr. Gordon knows that I told you about Black Israel."

"Who is Mr. Gordon?"

"The dark man in B drawing-room."

"Him?"

"Yessuh. He was asking me about Black Israel tonight. I told him I didn't know anything. You shouldn't have told him, Mr. Drake. I don't like his looks."

"Neither do I. And let me assure you I haven't told him anything and never will. Nor anybody else."

"Yessuh," he said with the ancient stolid grief of the Negro who has trusted a white and got his fingers burned, or smashed.

"I don't know why he was questioning you, but I had nothing to do with it. He couldn't have overheard us in the vestibule, because I watched for him—"

"You watched for him? Who is he, Mr. Drake?"

"I don't know. I'm going to try and find out. I don't like this any better than you do."

He went to make my berth, and I knocked on the door of drawing-room B. The dark man answered the door in his shirtsleeves. There were wrinkles in the left shoulder of his shirt which might have been made by the harness of a shoulder-holster.

"Mr. Gordon, I believe?"

"Mr. Drake, I know. Have you come to apologize?"

"I'll apologize when all the chips are down. What is your interest in Black Israel?"

"I am a sociologist."

"Can you prove that?"

"Certainly not. Is there any need to?"

"The need may arise."

"In that case I may as well tell you that I'm not a sociologist. Psychology interests me, however. At present I am attracted by the problem of you."

"You take the words out of my mouth, Mr. Gordon. I am fascinated by the problem of you."

"The problem of you is this," he said in a flat cold voice which harmonized with his flat cold eyes. "What curious hallucination has persuaded you that you can ask strangers personal questions, and even threaten them, without being sharply snubbed?"

He snapped the door shut in my face. I refrained from kicking it, but I had never felt less respect for the laws and conventions of civilized society. I went back to the smoking-room and smoked more cigarettes. Physical violence had beaten my impulses down to the animal level, and I craved more than anything else some physical outlet for my feelings. Yet I sat on my tail and for want of anything better to do, played a mental chess game in which half my men were missing and the board itself was in shadow, against an unknown antagonist who made three moves to my one.

My stalemated imagination rejected the illusion offered by the train's motion that I was getting somewhere. I was sick of its monotonous jerking, its idiot course along the line of least resistance to a predestined end. I felt boxed in and locked out.

After a long time Mary appeared at the door in her bathrobe. "Aren't you going to bed, Sam? It's very late. Besides, I don't like you sitting here by yourself."

"Sure. I'm going to bed."

The berths were all made and the curtains were drawn for the night. The ladder stood at my berth like an admonition.

I said, "Good night, Mary," and kissed her. Her body moved in toward me and her mouth grew soft. She said with her lips against mine: "Sam. Come in with me."

We lay together with the blind up and watched New Mexico unroll like a faded diorama. There was a faint moonlight which touched the earth with a greenish tinge, like a country at the bottom of the sea. The strange country which at high noon was a riot of pigmentation, a dead world brilliantly shadowed with post-mortem lividity, was at night an arid pasture of the moon. But because a girl's head was on my arm the shadowy country took female forms, was hung with a mysterious and sexual beauty.

"A train journey has a funny effect on me," Mary said. "I feel cut off from the real world, isolated and irresponsible. The time I spend on a train is like an interlude from real life."

"The country is Cockayne," I said. "Would you marry me if I asked you to?"

"Don't ask me that now," she said drowsily. "Pull down the shade and ask me if I love you in the dark."

That night I had no bad dreams.

At six a moral alarm clock clicked in my brain and woke me. Before I opened my eyes I could sense the warm fragrance of her breath and hear its quiet rhythm. When I opened them I could see the dim outline of her

132

closed face, pale and lustrous as a pearl in the early morning light. Moving cautiously so as not to disturb her, I retrieved my clothes and climbed out of the berth.

The passage between the green curtains was as deserted as a forest aisle, and as full of silence. A silence which held in suspension the rustlings and murmurs of hidden life. Periodically a long strangled snore fell through the silence like a falling tree. I hurried past the dangerous snore, but before I reached the end of the car a curtain moved and parted and a small agile figure in striped pyjamas climbed out backwards like a honeybear. I knew that the berth was Mrs. Tessinger's. The man, tousled, puff-eyed and cheerful-looking, was Teddy Trask.

He laid a finger on his lips and grinned sideways. I followed him to the men's room without speaking. There he said:

"Caught in the act. Oh, well."

"Sleep where you like. But I thought it was Rita you were working up to."

"So did I. For God's sake don't tell Rita I slept with her mother. She'd never speak to her again."

"It would be just as embarrassing for me as it would be for Rita."

"Yeah, and it would be twice as embarrassing for me. Oh, well."

I filled a washbowl with water and unwrapped a piece of soap. "I was under the impression that you liked them young."

"It didn't work out that way. Christ, I was practically raped. I guess it worked out all right, though. I can't complain."

The swirling water in the metal bowl seemed especially clear and hot. My senses were quick and appreciative. The rather sordid irony of Teddy Trask's affair with Mrs. Tessinger struck me as intensely amusing. I felt simultaneously alert and relaxed, ready for anything.

An hour or so later at early breakfast, I had a chance to ask Teddy for more information about his time code:

"You said you'd offered it to the Army Signal Corps. Could it be used on the radio, do you think?"

"I don't see why not," he said, sliding easily into his favorite subject. "You could go on the air and broadcast nothing but a tick every now and then. The enemy wouldn't even have to know you were broadcasting. But if they did, all they'd hear would be the same sound repeated at irregular intervals. That's where this code is different from any other code. The signals themselves don't mean anything. The meaning is in the time between them."

"We use the same principle in whistle signals. A six-second blast means one thing. A twelve-second blast means something else."

"That's right, it's the same principle," he admitted.

"Say the Army used your code. Wouldn't it take a long time to pass on a little information? And wouldn't the number of things you could say be pretty limited?"

He sipped his black coffee and lit a cigarette. "Sure, I admit that. That's probably the reason the Army turned it down. That and the fact that I wasn't a brass hat, or even a second lieutenant. But don't forget that you could work it out much finer on the air, with clocks synchronized to one-fifth of a second. That gives you five hundred meanings per one hundred seconds, if you take a fifth of a second as your unit."

"But then you'd still be limited to saying five hundred things and if your message was the five hundredth meaning you'd have to wait a hundred seconds between ticks. It would take you a hundred seconds to say it."

"That's right, too. It's slow. But I never thought it could be anything but a special-purpose code."

"And wouldn't an enemy cryptanalyst catch on pretty fast to your limited list of prearranged meanings?"

"That's where you're wrong, boy. Unless he had a time-sense better than any I've ever heard of, your enemy cryptanalyst wouldn't ever know he was listening to a code. That's the beauty of it. It could be used in guerrilla warfare, by advance agents in enemy country. But say your enemy cryptanalyst had an ear like a chronometer, or caught on some other way and started to time the ticks, you could still fool him."

134

"You could change your prearranged meanings at regular intervals, you mean?"

"Why not?" he said triumphantly. "You could change 'em every day. Say, you don't think the Navy would be interested in this, do you? I still think it's got possibilities."

"Maybe it has. I can't speak for the Navy. I can tell you what C.N.O. would say if you took it to them, though. They'd tell you it was fundamentally insecure because, in the first place, you know about it, and in the second place other people do. Me, for instance. Navy codes are originated by naval officers and by a few carefully chosen civilians, and they keep them under their hats."

"By God, I never thought of that." The light of triumph went out of his eyes like small sinking suns. "I've been shooting off my mouth all this time. Say, for all I know, maybe they've got it. Maybe they're using it right now, and I don't know anything about it."

"Maybe they are. I wouldn't know."

I left him with whatever vicarious fulfilment he could squeeze out of that. His ideas had suggested a possibility to me which seemed worth investigating. Sue Sholto had worked in a broadcasting station.

But the moldering body of Sue Sholto and the problem to which her dead face had introduced me were in the Territory of Hawaii, and I was on a train in Arizona. There was a more recent corpse and a more immediate problem to occupy my mind. Why had Hatcher died, assuming that it wasn't accident? And what, if any, were the relations between Hatcher and Anderson? Though I had no notion of what to do or say when I saw him, I sat in ambush in the club car waiting for Anderson to pass through to the diner, as if the mere sight of his face might suggest the key to the conundrum.

I waited a long time while the breakfast parade went by. Major Wright walking authoritatively on short legs. Rita Tessinger looking fresh and restless. Her mother with a complacent look of pleasant fatigue. The old lady from Grand Rapids armored in purple flowered silk against the menaces to her comfort which her quick old eyes found in

135

every corner. Finally Mary looking very young and beautiful, and deceptively virginal.

I told her about the first two and omitted the third.

"You're up early this morning," she said.

"I slept well last night."

"So did I. I dropped off as soon as my head hit the pillow."

"And I am the emperor's white horse and Halsey can ride me any time he wishes. I've already eaten breakfast. Shall I wait for you here?"

"Do."

She went away, her hips moving as if in gentle reminiscence. In a grey flannel dress her body had regained its mystery, and the cycle of desire began again in me.

It was interrupted by the appearance of Miss Green, alone, in a green dress the color of artificial Easter grass and matching green shoes. When she came nearer I could see that she had added jade earrings to her travelling exhibition of jewelry. She looked sick.

"Good morning," I said. "Have you seen Mr. Anderson this morning?"

"Didn't you know? Mr. Anderson got off the train."

"But he told me he was going through to L.A."

"Oh, he was. But he made a long-distance call to one of his oil-fields, and they told him he better stay in New Mexico for a couple of days. So last night, or I guess it was early this morning, he got off at Gallup. He told me he was going to Albuquerque."

"I wish I'd known. I would have liked to say good-bye to him. You don't have his California address, do you?"

"No, he said he moves around so much. He's got mine, though." She giggled hoarsely. "Well, I guess I'll go and see what they got for breakfast. See you later."

I felt blocked and yet, to a certain extent, vindicated. Perhaps my questions, which had seemed asinine at the time even to me, had frightened him off the train. If I could get the FBI in Los Angeles to cooperate with me, he could be found and asked those questions again.

I went back to the Pullman and asked the porter if Anderson had taken his bags with him.

"No, suh, he told Miss Green to tell me to put them in the baggage car. She said that he'll be going on to Los Angeles in a couple of days and they're to be held for him there. Mr. Gordon only had one bag and I guess he took that with him."

"Is Gordon gone too?"

"Yes, suh. It suits me."

"Did the two of them leave together?"

"I don't know, Mr. Drake. All I know is that they both got off at Gallup. Neither of them said a word to me."

Three possibilities occurred to me besides the one I had suggested. Gordon was following Anderson. Anderson was following Gordon. Or one had killed the other and bundled his body off the train. Actual melodrama and violence had accustomed my mind to move easily among melodramatic and violent possibilities. The melodrama of the situation deepened when I made inquiries and found out that nobody had seen Gordon or Anderson leave the train.

Miss Green and Mary came back from the diner together, and I asked Miss Green if Anderson had made arrangements for his luggage in advance.

"He left me a note. It was under my pillow when I woke up this morning. It was a very nice letter, not just a note."

"Are you sure he wrote it?"

"Of course I'm sure. Who else would write me a note?"

"Did you know his handwriting?"

"I don't know. No, I guess I don't. But I'm positive he wrote it. He said he was going to Albuquerque and to send his bags on to L.A."

"Had he mentioned getting off the train before?"

"No. I was surprised when I got his note."

"Where is it now?" I said.

"The note? Just a minute." She went to her compartment and searched it. But she came back empty-handed.

"It's gone," she said. "I can't understand it. I had it less than an hour ago."

The unreal painted flesh of her aging face hid her thoughts from me. I couldn't tell whether she was lying or not. Everything she said and did was artificial, slightly off the human center-line. The steady trembling of her hands was as if her nervous system had received a delicate and irreparable damage. A corpse returned to life after the tissues had decayed a little would have moved and spoken as she did, and had her taste in clothes.

Miss Green returned to her love-story magazines, and quickly became absorbed in a *Spicy Romances*. I went back to our compartment and sat down beside Mary.

"Miss Green wants to know if there's anything the matter," I said in a low voice. "If you ask me, there's something the matter with her."

"What do you mean? She's a type you see all over. An ignorant woman who got hold of money somewhere, and doesn't know how to use it on herself."

"Yeah, but how did she get her money?" I looked over my shoulder at Miss Green. Her fading prurient eyes were fastened on the pages of her pulp magazine. "There's something about her I don't like, something reptilian."

"Maybe she won it in a lottery," Mary said with a laugh. "Don't let your imagination run away with you, Sam. She's a pathetic old hag. I think I know women, and that's all I can see in her."

"She was pretty friendly with Anderson, too. I was beginning to feel there was something queer about him and now he's dropped out of sight. Too many people have been dropping through trap-doors. Gordon's gone, too."

"Gordon?"

"The man that was spying on you the other night in the club car. He left the train last night."

"Is that sinister? For all you know, he may have had a perfectly respectable reason—"

"Maybe he had. But I'm not taking it for granted. He acted fishy."

"Everything's looking fishy to you, Sam. Aren't you letting the whole thing get you down?"

"You're damn right I am. Can't you see we're both in this thing up to our necks? You or I may be the next to drop through the trap-door. I almost did."

"I know you did." She leaned towards me and put a firm

138

white hand on my knee. "Then why do you insist on stick-ing your neck out?"

"There's trouble in the air, and I believe in meeting trouble halfway. I want something to get hold of."

"But what if there isn't anything to get hold of?"

"A minute ago you said I was sticking my neck out. Now there's nothing to get hold of, and all this is my imagination. But I suppose I can't expect a woman to be logical."

"Maybe I'm not logical. I follow my feelings. And my feeling is that you should try to forget about this business."

I couldn't forget it, and I knew that she couldn't either, but I dropped the subject. My nerves were stretched and waiting, but there was nothing to do. I did my best to enjoy the long peaceful day.

We read and talked, intimate desultory talk. The train dragged itself across Arizona, spanned the Colorado gorge, spiralled up into the last great wall of mountains, slid down through blue-white light into the California coastal plain and the green season.

At ten-thirty that night the train stopped for the last time in the Los Angeles station, and we left it together. Climbing up the long sloping tunnel from the train, I had more than the usual feeling of strangeness on coming into an unfamiliar city. It was like climbing out of a tight little hell into an unpredictable chaos. Even my own intentions were unpredictable, but at the last minute I made up my mind.

"I'm going to Santa Barbara," I told Mary at the baggage counter.

"But you said you were coming to San Diego with me!" There was an angry flush in her cheeks. Her proprietary tone made me angry, too.

"I'm not," I said bluntly. "I may see you in Diego tomorrow night."

"What on earth are you going to Santa Barbara for?"

"I'm going to look up Laura Eaton. The girl Hatcher wrote the letter to."

She put her hand on my arm and drew me aside

from the crowd at the checking desk. "Please don't go, Sam. Stay in Los Angeles with me tonight."

"You're not jealous of a girl I've never seen?"

"I'm not jealous of anybody. I just don't want you to go to Santa Barbara. I'm afraid."

"Afraid of what?"

"What might happen to you. You mustn't go running around the country looking for trouble."

"I don't have to look for it. It found me long ago: I want to know what's in that letter, and I have to go to Santa Barbara to find out."

"And if I don't like I can lump it!" she said flatly.

She took her hand away from my arm. I felt very much alone.

PART IV

THE END OF THE RIDE

11

I LEFT her at the taxi-stand. She didn't say good-bye. I checked my bag through to San Diego, and took a northbound train. The hundred-mile journey in a coach was not pleasant. I was sick of trains anyway, and conflicting feelings were churning inside me. I hated to leave Mary standing, but unfinished events were tugging at me. I couldn't relax until I had done something, and the only feasible action I could think of was a visit to Laura Eaton, whoever she might be.

Between one and two in the morning I got off at the Santa Barbara station. The town had the salt smell of a seaport, but it was as dark and deserted as any prairie village in the middle of the night. I found a telephone book in a station booth and looked up Laura Eaton. There was a William Eaton at 2124 Bath Street.

I walked up the empty main street and finally captured a nocturnal taxi-driver dozing at the wheel. He took me out Bath Street. It was a quiet residential street of one-story stucco and frame houses nestling bone-white among palms and oleanders and flowering yews. To the right the mountains seemed to rise straight up behind them against the dim moonlit sky.

The mountains and the moonlight, the tropical trees and houses, the warm sea-laden wind which came in through the open windows of the cab reminded me of Oahu. I had a moment of false recognition as if I were riding to see the already seen, to find the already found: Sue Sholto hanging like a grotesque vine against a briefly moonlit wall. I had an intuition that I was completing an obscure and fearful cycle, but I had no sense of what the fulfilment would be.

Laura Eaton at least wore no rope around her neck. She greeted me at her door, which opened six inches on a chain, with a .38 revolver in her hand.

I said: "It looks as if they got here before I did."

"Put up your hands," she said in a voice which might have been pleasant under other circumstances. When I had done so, she unhooked the chain. "Now step inside while I call the police. If you make a false move I'll shoot you in the stomach."

She was a tall woman in her late twenties. Her tawny hair was down her back, matching the tan wool bathrobe which she wore. Holding her .38 steadily in her right hand she patted my pockets and armpits. She seemed surprised to find no gun, and looked at me for a moment without speaking.

"You're Laura Eaton, aren't you?"

"Yes. Who are you?"

"My name is Sam Drake. My friends call me Sam and always pull a gun on me when I knock on their door. It's a game we play."

"My house was entered today. I don't propose to have it entered again."

"But I've already entered it. Look. Now call the police."

She looked at me uncertainly. "Who are you anyway? Are you really in the Navy?"

"Do you know a man called Hatcher?"

"Rodney Hatcher?"

"I don't know his first name. He comes from Kansas City."

"That's Rodney."

"He died the night before last."

"He died! Is that why you've come, to tell me?" She had forgotten her gun. I lowered my hands.

"That's one reason. Point your gun away from my stomach, will you? It makes my stomach feel funny."

She clicked the safety and dropped the gun on the chesterfield, where it fell with a soft thump that was soothing to my nerves. "Why did you come at this time of night?" she said.

"I just got here. I came as soon as I could."

"Did Rodney send you? Tell me, what happened to Rodney?"

"He didn't exactly send me. He wrote you a letter just before he died. I thought it might have some bearing on his death. I came to you to find out."

"I haven't had a letter from him for weeks. Not since he wrote me from Europe that he was coming home for reassignment. How did he die? Was he wounded?"

"Were you and he very close?"

"We were good friends. I've known him off and on for years. We went to school together in Kansas City. You needn't pull any punches, if that's what you mean."

I told her briefly what had happened to Rodney Hatcher, not omitting my suspicions of Anderson and Gordon.

A few tears made shining tracks down her face, combining at the point of her chin to form a clinging drop of brine. She sat down on the edge of a chair and half turned away from me to use a handkerchief. "Poor Rodney," she said in a deep soft voice. "It was a beastly way to die."

"It was painless. You just go out like a light. I know from experience."

"It was beastly for him." She looked at me with fire and ice in her eyes. Her body was proud. I thought that Hatcher was lucky to have such a mourner. "He should have died in action. He should have died fighting."

"Who broke into your house today?" I said after a pause. "There may be a connection between that and Rodney's death."

"Do you think so? Do you think perhaps he was looking for Rodney's letter?"

"It seems very likely to me. Did you see what he looked like?"

"I didn't see him very well. I'll tell you what happened. This afternoon I ran over to Eva Raine's for an hour or so—she's a friend of mine who lives down the street."

"Had your afternoon mail come yet?"

"No, it came when I was gone. I started home about three. When I was about half a block from home I saw this man come down off my verandah. I didn't know then that he'd been in the house. I thought it was someone who had come to see me or father, so naturally I called to him and waved. He took one look at me over his shoulder and headed in the other direction, walking as fast as he could go.

"When I got home I found that the lock on my front door had been forced. The writing-desk had been ransacked and the bureaus and cupboards had been searched. I called the police and they said they'd hunt for him, but I haven't heard from them since. As a matter of fact, nothing was missing. I left my purse in the house in plain sight, and nothing in it was taken."

"You say your afternoon mail was there when you got home?"

"It was on the floor, right there." She pointed to the front door, which opened directly on the living-room where we were sitting. I turned my head and noticed that the door had a letter-slot in it. I also noticed that she had left it ajar.

"From the fact that he searched the house it looks as if Rodney's letter didn't come in that mail," I said. "It should be here tomorrow morning. It was mailed two days ago."

"If that man comes back I'll shoot him." Her full defiant lips pushed out, and her wide eyes became tigerish.

"I believe you will. Did you get any idea at all of what he looked like?"

"He was tall. He looked quite broad. The very first moment I thought it was father, but then I realized that father couldn't have gotten back from Phoenix so soon."

"Did he have black hair?"

"I'm not sure—" In the midst of her sentence she suddenly became quite still. Even her mouth was immobilized half open.

"It wasn't I, Mr. Drake, if that's what you're implying," a man's voice said from the direction of the door. I turned to see Gordon step quietly into the room with a contemptuously calm look in his black eyes.

146

I got up without haste and walked towards him. When I was near enough I dropped my right hand to the level of my knee and brought it up in an uppercut to the point of his long jaw. It was a sucker-punch, but he carried a gun. He went down with his back against the door, which slammed shut. Almost before he hit the floor there was a gun in his hand and I was looking into its round empty eye. The gun's eye followed me as he rose to his feet.

"That was hardly a fair blow," he said. His eyes were no longer calm. They were shining with malice. "I warned you to avoid violence, Mr. Drake."

"I'll show you a fair blow if you'll lower that gun. Maybe I will anyway."

"This gun is attuned to your aura, Mr. Drake. If you approach it it will go off."

There was a slight click behind me and Laura Eaton said: "I have you covered. Drop that gun."

Gordon's eyes did not move from me but his whole body tightened.

"I'll count to three before I shoot," she said. "One."

He turned the gun in his hand and handed it to me. "This is a ridiculous situation," he said.

"Not as ridiculous as it's going to be," I said. "Miss Eaton, will you call the police."

"You needn't bother," Gordon said. "I am the police."

"You change identities with breath-taking rapidity. Go ahead, Miss Eaton. I've got him covered now."

Gordon reached for his hip pocket.

"Keep your hands in sight," I said sharply. "Put them on your head."

"Very well, if that appeals to your boyish sense of fun." He raised his hands, grinning at me sardonically. "Take my wallet out of my left hip pocket. You'll find my identity card in it."

I circled around him with his body at the hub of my line of fire and secured his wallet. It contained a card which identified him as Chester Gordon, Special Agent of the Federal Bureau of Investigation. I felt cheated, doubtful and angry. My melodrama had descended into

147

farce, and all the wasted adrenalin turned sour in my veins.

"I'm sorry to have spoiled your game of cowboys and Indians," Gordon said acidly. "Now put down that gun, or it may get you into trouble."

"You could have stolen this FBI card," I said uncertainly.

"Put down that gun," he said with authority. "Hefler wouldn't like it if you shot me by accident."

I remembered the smooth-talking red-haired man in the FBI office on Lafayette Street. "Are you working for Hefler?"

"I could arrest you for assaulting me, Mr. Drake. You've acted like a damn fool."

I lowered the gun. He took his hands from his head and stroked his bruised jaw.

"I'm not in a mood for apologizing," I said bitterly. "If you had taken me into your confidence—"

"We don't take the general public into our confidence when we're working on a case."

"God damn it, there wouldn't be any case if it weren't for me!"

"I'd be just as happy," Laura Eaton said, "if you men wouldn't stage another brawl in my living-room. We're all three on the same side, aren't we?"

Gordon said, "Excuse me."

Further recriminations rose from my wounded feelings to my lips: If you had cooperated with me we might have been able to save Hatcher, we might have been able to trap Anderson. But I swallowed them and held my tongue. I could see his point. An investigator of murder and espionage had to work in secrecy, especially in the cramped intimacy of a train.

I said, "Excuse me," to Laura Eaton. To Gordon: "What were you doing on the train? You weren't checking up on me, by any chance?"

"I was there partly to protect you. Two deaths had coincided with your presence. It looked as if the trouble was following you. After Hatcher died I was certain of it."

I couldn't resist saying: "Your protection didn't do me much good. Nor Hatcher."

"I could hardly serve as your food-taster, Mr. Drake. Nor am I ubiquitous."

"You're ubiquitous enough to suit me. What brought you here tonight?"

"After Hatcher was killed, my suspicions narrowed on Anderson. I did my best to shadow him. When you jumped me at the door of the smoking-compartment last night I think he caught on. He got off the train at Gallup and I followed him, but not fast enough. He took the only available taxi to Albuquerque, and I had to wait for the train to leave. When I got to Albuquerque he had already gone.

"I traced him to the airfield and found that he had chartered a plane to Los Angeles. I took the first commercial flight but when I got to L.A. there was no trace of him there. Like you, I got the idea that he might have come to Santa Barbara to intercept Hatcher's letter to Miss Eaton. I flew up here at noon and found that he had. He landed at the Santa Barbara airport this morning, and disappeared. Only Miss Eaton has seen him since. The local police informed me of the entry into her house this afternoon. Since then I've been watching this house. The local police are watching the roads in and out of town."

"I didn't realize I had a bodyguard," Laura Eaton said. "It feels nice. I don't know as much about handling a gun as I pretended to."

"Our organization exists for the protection of the public," Gordon said sententiously.

"I suppose you know all the circumstances of Bessie Land's death?" I said.

Laura Eaton leaned forward in her seat and looked at me curiously, but had enough character to hold her tongue.

"I've been over the evidence with Hefler," Gordon said. "As a matter of fact, I examined the cadaver."

"Do you agree with the police that it was suicide?"

"No, I don't. Some of those municipal police are

textbook-ridden. They've learned that hesitation-marks are often associated with suicide, so whenever they see a hesitation-mark they jump to the conclusion that it's suicide. In this case, a more likely hypothesis is that Bessie Land was murdered while in an alcoholic coma. The tissues of her brain were saturated with alcohol."

"I saw her a couple of hours before she died. She was terribly drunk then."

"Exactly. It's quite likely that the killer hesitated in the act of murder and made a shallow cut in her throat before he could gather enough courage to complete the act. Alcohol is an anaesthetic, and Bessie wouldn't necessarily be aroused. That's one way of accounting for the hesitation-mark. Another way, and I consider this more probable, is that it was deliberately inflicted to make the murder look like suicide. That would call for almost surgical coolness, and for some knowledge of medico-legal doctrine. But I think the criminals we're dealing with are cool enough and intelligent enough. Besides, murder arranged to look like suicide fits in with the previously established pattern."

"You mean Sue Sholto's murder?"

"Sue Sholto's murder?" Laura Eaton said in a shocked whisper.

"There have been three murders," Gordon said. "Your friend Hatcher was the third."

Laura Eaton's face became pale and her body seemed to grow smaller. She put her hands over her face.

"You spoke of criminals," I said. "In the plural."

"There doesn't seem to be any doubt that we're up against an organization—"

"Black Israel?"

"Black Israel is part of the organization, or associated with it. I got a wire when the train stopped in Kansas City. They've picked up the Negro who was sitting beside Bessie Land the night she was killed—"

"I knew he had something to do with it."

"He didn't kill her," Gordon said. "He proved that he remained in the Paris Bar and Grill continuously until after 2 A.M., and she was dead long before that. But he is a member of Black Israel. He broke down and confessed."

"Are the Japs behind it?"

"If they are, he doesn't know, or won't admit it. He did admit that Black Israel takes a passive-resistance stand on the war effort. As a matter of fact, his own draft status was not what it should be. That's the charge we're holding him on. He's given us some leads, and we're rounding up the leaders. Hector Land was a minor leader and a comparatively recent member, he said. And he mentioned a white man who supplied Black Israel with funds for propaganda purposes."

"Anderson."

Gordon leaned back and lit a cigarette. "I think so."

There was still tension between us, like an electric arc whose contact points were my sore knuckles and Gordon's bruised jaw. I said sharply: "If you thought so, why didn't you arrest him on the train?"

His black eyes gave me a cold superior stare. "For the simple reason that I had no legal evidence against him. You don't seem to realize how the police must work in a democratic country, Drake. During this war, our Bureau has watched known criminals for as long as two or three years without acting to arrest them. Watched them every minute of every day for years, waiting for something to give them away. In the end, something always does. A slip of the tongue, an error in planning, a chance meeting—"

"It was the chance meeting with Hatcher that gave Anderson away," I said. "Hatcher said he knew Anderson, or at least implied it."

"That may be so. Perhaps his letter will give us the clue we need, the reason for his death."

Laura Eaton said: "Goodness, I could do with a cup of coffee. My head's simply spinning. What about you gentlemen?"

We said we would, and she started for the kitchen.

Before she disappeared Gordon said: "What time is your morning mail delivery?"

"Usually about nine o'clock. Do you think he'll be back?"

151

"I don't know. He's a tricky customer. He may be too wary to try it again. I'm going to wait and find out."

"I'm going to wait, too," I said. "If I may borrow Miss Eaton's chesterfield and gun for the rest of the night."

"You may," she said from the kitchen door. In a minute there was the sound of water rushing from a faucet into a coffee percolator.

We waited in silence for a while. My anger had drained away leaving dregs of shame in my system, and some alarm at my temerity. I felt considerable awe of the Federal Bureau of Investigation. And I realized how easily he could have shot me.

My glance fell on an electric record-player beside a lamp in the corner. The albums of records in its cabinet switched my mind to a track that it had been following earlier that day. I said:

"I realize that you have a low opinion of my investigative talents. I realize that you're somewhat justified, and that the smartest thing I've done was to go to the FBI. But I have an idea that I think you should hear."

"It was partly my fault that we worked at cross-purposes," he admitted. "But I don't see how it could have been helped. What's your idea?"

"It's nothing better than a hunch. It may be completely screwy. Hefler must have told you that secret information was leaking out of Hawaii to the enemy. At least that's what I was told."

"I knew it before Hefler told me. We've known about it for a couple of months."

"But you haven't been able to put your finger on the leak. Teddy Trask, the magician who put on an act in the club car that first afternoon, told me about a code which he and his partner had developed—"

"I heard him talking about it. I was there."

"That's right, you were. The principle of that code could be used by an enemy agent working in a commercial broadcasting station. Sue Sholto, the girl who was hanged—"

"I know about her," he said impatiently. "How could it be used?"

"Sue Sholto broadcast regularly from Honolulu, and there was nothing to prevent Japanese subs from picking up her broadcasts. She could have sent out information in the course of an apparently innocent program."

"Commercial broadcasts are monitored. We would have caught it."

"Not if she used a code like Teddy Trask's. She could mark her records with a needle so that they'd give out a little click at prearranged intervals. The time elapsed between clicks would have a definite meaning. A monitor, if he noticed the sounds at all, would think it was nothing but a worn record."

"I admit that's possible. But you've got nothing to go on."

"That's why I'm telling you. I can't check on it myself. But you can teletype your office in Honolulu and ask them to examine the record library in the radio station."

"It's worth trying, I suppose. It sounds outlandish. But their system must be outlandish, whatever it is, or we'd have gotten on to it long ago."

Laura Eaton came back with coffee and sandwiches. Gordon drank his coffee in a hurry and got up to leave:

"I'm going over to the Marine Base and put that dispatch on the wires. It's not likely that Anderson will come back before morning anyway."

"I hope he does," I said. "I've gone to target practice on the fantail every afternoon for a year."

"When I come back I won't come into the house. Lay low for an hour after the mailman gets here. Keep the doors and windows locked."

Laura Eaton retired to her own room. After turning out the lights I lay down on the chesterfield with her revolver in my hand and waited for morning. I dozed intermittently, held on the edge of sleep by coffee and fear. Morning came very slowly, leaking between the slats of the Venetian blinds, pale and bluish like watered milk. By seven o'clock the coffee and fear had worn off and I fell into a light sleep. I awoke with a start at nine when three letters plopped through the slot in the door and slid across the waxed floor.

153

I crawled across the floor to the letters keeping my head below the level of the windows. Hatcher's posthumous message was among them.

I returned to the chesterfield with it, ripped open the envelope, and read at the end of the letter:

"P.S.—I should have mailed this before I left K.C., I want it to get to you before I do or there'll be hell to pay. But a bunch of the boys—remember Alvin S. and Donnie Hope?—kept me in a bar until the last minute and I didn't have a chance. Anyway I got me a bottle to nurse on the train. I met a naval ensign who seems like a right guy and he had some good bourbon but it's all gone now. He lent me this pen in case you wonder why the ink is different—I don't know what happened to mine. Christ, it was the one you sent me, too.

"There's a guy on the train I don't like the looks of. Remember that white man I told you about that was handling black market rice in Nanking when the Japs were there? This guy is either him or his brother, and I'm going to find out which. This guy is older and fatter but if it isn't the same guy then it's a case of identical twins. He says his name is Anderson. I don't think he knows me.

"Well, so long for now. You'll hear from me when I get to L.A., and I'm going to do my damnedest to get to see you before I ship out. I should have written before but you know how it is. Bob and Dee send their regards. R.H."

12

I WAITED for another hour, ready to shoot Anderson if he appeared. Punctually at ten o'clock there was the sound of feet on the verandah and I looked through the Venetian blind and saw Gordon at the door. Before I opened it to him Laura Eaton came out of her bedroom fully dressed. She had the marks of sleeplessness on her face.

"I think we can assume that he won't be back," Gordon said. "But I'll have the local police keep an eye on your house, Miss Eaton. Just in case."

"Did Rodney's letter come?" she said.

"I hope you don't mind my opening it. There's not much doubt that Anderson killed him. And dragged me under the train."

I handed her the letter, and Gordon read it over her shoulder.

"May I have this letter?" Gordon said.

"Of course. Won't you let me make you some more coffee?"

"Thank you. But I've got to get going."

"Did you send your message to Honolulu?" I said.

"Yes. I told them to rush an answer. If you need to get in touch with me, call our central office in Los Angeles. I'll give them your name. Where will you be?"

"I've got a reservation at the Grant in San Diego. I'm going to San Diego today."

"I may see you there. I understand Hector Land's ship is in San Diego, and I intend to go aboard her."

"So do I."

He shook hands with me and Laura Eaton and went out the door. I wondered when he slept.

I turned to Laura Eaton and asked if I could use her phone.

"Certainly. There in the hall. Is this Anderson a spy, or something like that?"

"Something like that. I'd tell you more, but the FBI asked me not to."

"I know as much as I want to," she said. "I'll make you some coffee."

I called the local airline office and added my name to their cancellation list. After breakfast with Laura Eaton I taxied out to the airfield on spec, and managed to get a seat on the next plane to Burbank. There I had a long wait for the San Diego plane. I called Mary's hotel and was told that she had checked out, leaving me a message to meet her in San Diego.

The afternoon seemed to be holding its breath. I paced the waiting room, tried to read a newspaper, saw Anderson and murder between the lines, got up and paced again. I tried to call Gordon at the FBI office but he hadn't been there. I watched the planes from the north and east drop down unarmed out of the sky like harmless hawks. From one a female movie star emerged and grinned starkly at a starkly grinning flashbulb.

I watched the soft-bodied stern-faced executives, the wealthy enameled women who commuted from coast to coast, the brass hats rubbing gold-heavy sleeves with casual soldiers and nonchalant seamen, sucked back from leave by the maelstrom in the Pacific. Parting couples embraced in the last agony of separation; reunited couples met and embraced in a similar agony of delight. I thought continuously of Anderson hustling somewhere across the southwestern states, sowing evil with jovial and expansive gestures.

A few minutes before my plane was due I called Gordon again and this time I got him.

"I'm glad you called," he said. "But I thought you were going to San Diego."

"I'm waiting for my plane now. Any trace of Anderson?"

"A man answering to his description registered at a motel near Delmar last night, under the name of Isaac Randall. He drove away in the direction of San Diego. Of course it may not be the man we want, but we'll get Anderson. We've telegraphed his description all over the southwestern states, and the state police are on the lookout for him."

"You haven't heard from Honolulu yet?"

"No. I'm expecting to anytime. I'll give them another hour or so, and then fly down to San Diego. I want to talk to Lieutenant Swann. His ship's still there."

"Are you going aboard tonight?"

"If I get away in time."

"I'll see you then."

"Right." He hung up.

When I opened the door of the phone booth the loudspeaker system was announcing that the San Francisco plane was about to land. I went outside and watched it come in and taxi down the field.

The second man out of the door in the side of the plane, which was almost too narrow for his bulk, was Gene Halford. He had shed his correspondent's uniform and was wearing bright new California clothes. But he had the same old face, and it gave me no pleasure to see it again.

I stepped back from the gate, intending to let him pass without speaking. But before he went by his glance fell on my face. I thought that his heavy body became a little awkward and self-conscious under his new clothes, and I didn't go out of my way to put him at ease:

"You were only half a civilian before. I see you decided to go the limit."

He flushed and said: "It's not my own choice. My syndicate wants me to write background material for the big international conference that's on its way. So that's what I'm writing." Then he remembered his sense of importance: "Not that it's any pressing concern of yours."

"I'd hate to feel it was."

Halford moved toward me out of the line of passengers which he had been obstructing. There was a vague threat in the way he held his heavy shoulders. "Look here, whatever your name is," he said. "I've had about enough of your gratuitous unpleasantness. I haven't forgotten that you took a girl away from me that night in Honolulu."

"Neither have I. It's one of my pleasanter memories."

"It is, is it? What would you think if I told you the girl was simply sorry for you?"

"I'd think you have more imagination than brains."

"I don't happen to be depending on my imagination. I spent an evening with Miss Thompson in San Francisco a week or so ago. A very pleasant evening."

If I kept hurt surprise out of my face, it was because I'd played a lot of poker. "I expect to see her in an hour," I said. "I'll ask her about that evening and probably we'll both have a good laugh."

"Why, where is she?"

"Out of your reach. So long."

I walked past him and up the ramp into the plane. The plane roared, sprinted and took flight. As we went up, the horizon spread out to include many mountains and wide blue meadows of ocean. But my whole mind was involved in a tight little knot of jealousy which wouldn't come loose. Anderson and his nasty business dropped out of my thoughts. Throughout the short flight to San Diego and the long taxi ride from Lindbergh Field to the Grant Hotel, my mind stayed on Mary and Gene Halford.

I found her in her room. When she opened the door she said, "Darling! I'm so glad to see you," and kissed me on the mouth.

After a minute the knot inside me loosened a little and I kissed her back. Then I held her away from me and looked into her eyes. They were transparent and bottomless, like deep water where men have drowned.

She laughed with charming girlishness. "You're awfully solemn, Sam. Are you still thinking?"

"Look," I said. "I take you seriously. Can you get that through your head? As seriously as hell."

A warm emotion swam up from the shadowy depths of her eyes. But she said, "Really?" with smiling lips.

"I just said it. I didn't say it before."

"I wondered if you ever would."

158

"But get this. If I take you seriously I expect to be taken seriously myself. I met Gene Halford for a minute at the Burbank airport."

"So? I suppose he told you I went out with him in San Francisco."

"That's right. I didn't like the idea. You told me in Pearl you barely knew him. And you didn't tell me you saw him in Frisco. I don't like him."

"Neither do I," she said demurely.

"You go out with him. And it's important enough to you that you didn't tell me about it."

"Don't be silly, Sam. I went out with him once. We just happened to meet the night our transport docked. I didn't tell you because I was afraid you'd get irrational about it. Just like you are getting."

"Sure I'm irrational. I'm irrational about anything with you in it."

She touched my cheek with her fingers. I caught her hand and kissed its palm. She said, "Please look at it sensibly, Sam. When I came back from Honolulu I had no way of knowing I'd ever see you again. Gene Halford has a lot of important contacts in the radio business. He does a lot of broadcasting himself. Well, I'll probably be going back into radio after the war. I'd be stupid if I didn't make the most of my chances."

"Do you think you can use Halford? Anything you get out of him you'll pay for."

"I know. I found that out."

"What do you mean?"

"I mean that anything I get out of Halford I'll pay for. There aren't many men that isn't true about."

"Is that a crack?"

"How could it be?" She smiled with deceptive sweetness. "I haven't got anything out of you."

I was taking a beating, and I knew it. I said unpleasantly: "Yeah, they pay the boys that write about it a hell of a lot more than the boys that do it."

That broke her down. She moved in to me. "Let's not quarrel, Sam. I detest the man. You and I got along so well from the beginning. At least, I thought we did."

159

My arms accepted her. "I know. Better than with any girl I've known."

"It's these terrible things that happened that changed things. You've changed, darling." Her face was against me and her voice was muffled. "We mustn't let things like that break us up."

"Breaking up is a long way from what I had in mind. I didn't know you were planning to go back into radio after the war. I thought maybe you were starting to have other plans. I was starting."

"Plans with you?" she said.

"Did you think I was playing?"

"I didn't know. Sam, do you really mean what you just said?"

"What did I just say? You make me dizzy standing so close."

"That we could have a postwar plan together?"

"I didn't know whether I could ask you. It's hard to look ahead very far. My survivor leave will be over in a few days. And maybe next time I won't be a survivor."

"Don't say it. You couldn't die."

"Everybody can die. A good many have. You'd have to take a chance on waiting."

She smiled very sweetly. "Maybe it's worth a chance. You look pretty durable. You look pretty, period."

"Pretty is a lousy word for a man. Get this straight, though. If we start waiting for each other, no playing around with anybody else. That goes for both of us. My last girl tried it, and she couldn't hold out."

"That hurt you, didn't it?"

"It's where the war hit me hardest."

"I wouldn't be catching you on the rebound, would I?"

"Maybe you would. Emotions are as strange as anything. Especially mine. If emotions weren't so strange I think I'd want to marry you tomorrow."

"I couldn't." She looked at me quickly.

"Why not?"

"Tomorrow's my first day on my new job. I couldn't take off my first day to get married, could I?"

"There isn't anybody else, is there? Not Halford or anybody?"

"Can't you see I'm mad about you, Sam?" Her body said the rest, and its language was irresistible.

After a time I told her about my night in Santa Barbara, and Hatcher's letter.

"Sam, I told you you were playing with fire. Promise me you won't risk it any more. I didn't sleep at all last night."

"I'm extremely crazy about you," I said. "But I'm even crazier about the idea of seeing Anderson again. Anyway, I never did like the idea of sitting and waiting for somebody else's axe to fall."

She looked at me with a drooping mouth. I kissed her mouth. Then I sat down on the edge of the bed to phone Eric Swann on his destroyer. She sat behind me and put her arms around me.

In the time between my dialling and the operator's answer from the Naval Repair Base, I said: "The girl loves me."

"Yes, I do. More than you love me."

"That's impossible. You're much more loveable than I am."

The operator answered and I asked for the appropriate extension.

Mary's teeth closed lightly on the back of my neck. "Don't argue or I'll really bite. You know you don't love me as much as I love you."

The Officer of the Deck on the destroyer answered, and I asked for Lieutenant Swann.

"I'm not sure whether he's aboard. Wait a minute, please."

I turned to kiss Mary and her lips clung, parting over mine. The world narrowed to a small burning circle.

The receiver, which had dropped on the bed, said in a cracked remote voice: "Lieutenant Swann speaking."

I swam up out of warm forgetful depths and talked back to him. "This is Sam. How about asking me out for dinner."

"Sure. How are you? I thought you were still in Detroit."

"Just got in today. Can I bring Mary aboard?"

"I'm sorry, Sam. No civilians allowed on the Repair Base. Do you still want to come?"

"Yes. We've got things to talk about. Hector Land hasn't been picked up yet, has he?"

"No, he's dropped clean out of sight. We eat at seven in port. Call the ship from the main gate and I'll send a jeep for you."

"Right." I set the receiver down.

I stood up and said to Mary: "Well, here I go again."

"Damn it. You were going to have dinner with me." Her voice was quietly furious.

"I'm awfully sorry. I'll get back as soon as I can. I should be able to make it between nine and ten o'clock."

"I'll be waiting for you, I suppose. Though you deserve to be stood up."

I took a taxi out to the Repair Base. When it dropped me at the gate I saw Chester Gordon standing in the roadway by the guards' kiosk talking to the Marine guard.

When I approached the guard looked at my I.D. card, saluted with characteristic Marine elegance and fervor, and moved away.

"What's the word?" I said to Gordon.

He smiled less grimly than he had smiled before. "The pieces are falling into place. Your hunch was good, Drake. A number of the records in the radio station's record library were marked as you thought they might be. It's evident that those records were deliberately prepared for the purpose of sending out coded intelligence. I didn't get the details, but they'll send an amplifying report when they've made a more complete investigation. What do you know about this Sue Sholto?"

"Not very much. She was reticent. Even her best friend didn't know much about her. Lieutenant Swann can tell you more than I can. He'd known her for a long time."

"I was just talking to Swann on the phone. He promised to send over a jeep for me, but there seems to be a holdup."

162

"I'll ride with you if I may. I'm going aboard for dinner."

"I don't think I've eaten for twenty-four hours or more. Things have been popping so fast. We got a teletype from Chicago—I sent them Anderson's description because that's where he got on the train. A man approximating his description, Lorenz Jensen by name, was convicted of contributing to the delinquency of a minor in Chicago in 1934. He served two years and four months of a five year sentence in Joliet."

"Did he escape?"

"No, he was released on parole. But he violated his parole and disappeared. Presumably he left the country."

"Anderson was in China in 1936. That tallies."

"It's pretty uncertain. You can never go by description alone, especially after a lapse of ten years. But fingerprints are another matter, and I've requested Chicago to send me photostats of Jensen's prints by airmail. Jensen's and Anderson's prints are in the same classification, we know that much."

"Did Anderson leave his prints in Laura Eaton's house?"

"No, he must have worn gloves. We got them out of his luggage in the baggage room of the Los Angeles station. He left a beautiful set of the thumb and first three fingers of the right hand on a bottle of shaving lotion. That's the only revealing thing he did leave in his luggage."

"When you boys move," I said, "you move fast and in all directions."

"We've got the organization, and that's something amateurs don't have. I don't mean that your help hasn't been extremely useful. We've depended more on lay assistance in this war than we've ever admitted in the papers."

"The word amateur carries no sting for me," I said. "This looks like our transportation now."

We rode in a jeep to the dock where the destroyer was berthed. Eric met us at the gangway, and I introduced him to Gordon:

"I think Mr. Gordon would appreciate an invitation to dinner. Though he seldom eats or sleeps."

"I should warn you about pot-luck," Eric said. "It's always pot-luck on this can."

"I've never been aboard a warship before," Gordon said. "It'll be very romantic to eat salt pork and hardtack, and drink a noggin of brackish water."

We had a steak dinner which Gordon and I punished severely, then retired to the privacy of Eric's stateroom. Gordon outlined the development of the case and concluded:

"I hope you won't think we're jumping to conclusions, because we're not. But it's in the cards for me to ask you what you know about Sue Sholto. Naturally a thorough investigation is being made in Honolulu. In the meantime it's up to me to find out what I can at this end. Anderson is at this end, and Hector Land is, or was. Can you tell me anything that might link Sue Sholto with Hector Land, or with a man that might be Anderson, or with the apparently subversive activities of those two?"

I had been watching Eric's face while he listened to Gordon's careful lecture. The last month had changed him. When I met him in Honolulu on the day of the party, it had seemed to me that he was suspended between acceptance and rejection of the world. His eyes had been turned outward, but uncertainly. His face had begun to set in the closed, bound look of a neurotic egotism. But the process had seemed then to be susceptible of interruption. Now the process was complete.

His smiles were no longer spontaneous, his looks were not naïve. The center of his being had retired into a secret labyrinth where it sat like a spider, clutching its means with avarice and regarding its ends with narrow passion. In a word, grief and shock are not always ennobling. Eric thought of the death of Sue Sholto chiefly as a possible obstacle in his naval and postnaval career and a thorn in his comfort.

"I didn't know her very well," he said. "She was just a girl I dated a few times. Naturally if I had any reason to suspect her of illegal activities I'd have reported her. Certainly I'd have had nothing more to do with her."

"There was no sign of a relationship between her and Hector Land?"

"Certainly not. And so far as I know she wasn't acquainted with anyone who might have been Anderson."

"Isn't it true that she was politically suspect?" I said. "Mary described her as a fellow-traveller."

"I wouldn't know. We never discussed politics."

Gordon put in: "Did she show curiosity about naval affairs?"

"The normal feminine curiosity, I suppose. She didn't ever try to pump me that I can remember."

"How long did you know the girl?"

"A few months. But I was at sea most of the time, and only dated her a few times when I was in port. She had other friends. I don't see why I should be singled out merely because I was with her on the night she killed herself." His voice was bitter.

"You aren't being singled out, Lieutenant Swann. You simply happen to be available for questioning. Did you know any of her other friends?"

"No, I never met any of them. She just mentioned them occasionally. I don't remember any names. And I very much hope that you'll keep my name out of this when it breaks in the papers. I have a wife in Michigan and if—"

"I know what you mean. Let me assure you we have no desire to embarrass innocent parties." As Eric became more reticent and cautious, Gordon became smoother and more glib, like a salesman who has lost a sale but wishes to retain the goodwill of the customer.

"Mary could tell you more than Eric," I said to Gordon. "She worked with Sue Sholto and was friendly with her. One woman can find out things about another woman more easily than a man can, anyway."

"I'll get in touch with her tomorrow. Where is she staying?"

"At the Grant for the present. But I think you'll have to depend on your Honolulu sources for the bulk of your evidence. I gather that Sue Sholto didn't talk about herself."

"I was about to come to this end of the affair," Gordon said in a faintly patronizing tone. "Lieutenant Swann, can you round up two or three members of the crew who were intimate with Land?"

"I don't think he was intimate with anybody. But I'll see what I can do. Do you want to wait here?"

"If you don't mind my using your room."

"Not at all." Eric went out.

He returned in about ten minutes with two Negroes. In the interval Gordon cross-questioned me about the circumstances of Sue Sholto's death. He was particularly interested in the movements of the guests and of Hector Land, which I reconstructed from memory as well as I could.

The two Negroes who preceded Eric unwillingly through the hatch looked frightened. They exchanged furtive looks. Their mouths were closed and set. Gordon's introduction of himself capitalized on their fear:

"My name is Gordon. I am an agent of the Federal Bureau of Investigation. My special field is subversive activities, that is, catching spies and traitors."

"This is Joe Doss, the Captain's steward," Eric said. Joe Doss was a small fat man with an almost hairless head and the face of a dusky moon. "This is Albert Feathers, one of the mess-boys who shared a compartment with Land." Albert Feathers was a lanky mulatto with large liquid eyes, a convulsive Adam's apple, and hair that was forcibly straight.

"Hector Land," Gordon continued, "is suspected of being a spy and a traitor. He was apparently a member of an illegal organization named Black Israel. Did he ever mention it to you?"

"No, sir. He never mentioned anything like that to me." Joe Doss disowned Hector Land in the same spirit, almost the same words, that Eric had used in disowning Sue Sholto: "I didn't know him very well. He worked down in the wardroom and I worked up in the Captain's galley."

"Feathers, you went on liberty with Land more than once," Eric said.

"Yes, sir," Feathers admitted in a dull voice. "But I wouldn't have nothin' to do with his lodge."

"Did he try to get you to join Black Israel?" Gordon said.

"Yes, sir. He didn't call it Black Israel, but that must be what he was talking about. He said it was to make the dark people strong."

"By what methods?"

"He didn't say. I told him he was just going to get himself into trouble, and when I told him that he just shut up like a clam. He said he'd get me if I said anything to anybody."

"You should have told me or your division officer about that," Eric said. "You might have saved a lot of trouble."

"Yes, sir," he said tonelessly. "I'll know better next time."

"Did Hector Land try to persuade you to spy for him?"

"Oh, no, sir, nothing like that. He didn't say anything about me spying. He just told me about the secret society. I just thought it was like an ordinary secret society." Feathers' large eyes seemed ready to dissolve in tears. His feet were rooted to the floor but his long body moved restlessly under his blue dungarees.

"Where did Hector Land get his money?"

"I don't know, sir. He got his pay."

"I'm not talking about his pay. He had more money than the Navy ever paid him. Where did he get it?"

"I don't know, sir. Maybe he got it spying."

"Why you making that up, Albert?" Joe Doss said. "You don't know if he made his money spying."

"No, sir. I thought that's what you meant."

"Hector Land made money gambling," Joe Doss said.

"Yes, sir," Feathers echoed. "He made money gambling. He ran a pool. He told me one time that back in Detroit he used to be overlook man for a policy wheel."

Gordon turned to Doss, who seemed the more intelligent of the two: "What kind of a pool?"

"I don't know, sir. It was some kind of a numbers game."

"Did you ever buy a chance in it?"

"No, sir, I don't gamble."

"We're not interested in checking up on gambling just now," Eric said. "If you know anything, let's have it. You won't suffer for it. It may do you some good."

A flicker of hopefulness passed over Feathers' sullen brown face. "I know what kind of a pool it was, sir. It was a ship pool. All the dark boys bought chances in it. Not just on the ship. On the beach, too."

"What is a ship pool?" Gordon said.

"Well, all the ships have numbers and if a ship came in with our number we won."

Gordon straightened up in his chair as if someone had pressed a trigger in his spine. But his voice was almost casual when he said:

"I'm not sure I understand. You mean that Hector Land based his numbers game on the goings and comings of naval vessels in Pearl Harbor?"

"Yes, sir. When we were in Frisco he had the pool, too."

"That's impossible!" Eric said angrily. "Only officers have access to that information."

"Where did Land get his information?" Gordon said.

"We could see the ships, sir," Feathers said. "Everybody knows what ships are in. And he could always check up on the daily Ships Present list."

"That's a lie," said Joe Doss, like the Chinaman who wrote on the wall where he had hidden his money that there was no money hidden there.

"I didn't say anything about you, Joe," said Albert Feathers, like the other Chinaman who wrote on the wall after he had stolen the money that he personally was innocent of the theft.

Eric turned on Joe Doss. "Have you been messing with the Captain's Ships Present list?"

"No, sir, I don't ever mess with anything on the Captain's desk." Drops of sweat came out on his high black forehead like globules of rendered fat. He swivelled a swift revengeful look at Albert Feathers.

"I want these men to make a deposition," Gordon said to Eric. "This evidence is of first-rate importance."

"You're damned right it is. I'll have to take the matter up with the Captain, but there'll be no difficulty there." He looked at Doss. "There's another matter I'll take up with the Captain at the same time. Doss, you're coming with me to see the Master-at Arms."

Doss followed him out on hopeless legs. Feathers stood where he was, apparently occupied with intimations of disaster.

"You may go, Feathers," Gordon said. "I'll want to get in touch with you in the morning. If you've told a straight story and continue to tell one you have nothing to fear." The faint trace of ham in his nature added with dramatic effectiveness: "The United States Government will appreciate your assistance."

"Don't talk this around," I said before Feathers left the room.

Gordon turned to me with a tense smile. "By God, this case is breaking. Now to give the Mexican police a shot in the arm. We've got to get our hands on Land."

"Land had a smooth way of gathering information. I wonder if he thought that up himself. He didn't strike me as particularly bright."

"I doubt it. There are real brains behind this business, Drake. With the possible exception of the Schneider case, this is the trickiest business I've worked on in this war. Schneider had the brains, but he was a piker compared with this outfit. This is nothing less than a conspiracy to give the Japs the whole outline of our naval movements in the Pacific."

I said not without complacence: "I've suspected it for a hell of a long time."

"The pattern is beginning to emerge," Gordon said. "As I see it it's something like this. Hector Land collected information which he passed on to another agent in Honolulu. It's unlikely that he was the only one supplying information, but he's the only one we know about so far. The second agent—"

"Sue Sholto?"

169

"Perhaps. We haven't enough evidence to say certainly yet. The second agent sifted the information, encoded the significant items, and broadcast them via the marked records to be picked up by Nip submarines lying off the Islands. The information was then re-encoded and relayed to Tokyo, or it may have been taken to Wake Island for rebroadcast."

"But where does Anderson come in?"

"Probably on the administrative end. He coordinated the whole thing from the mainland. There doesn't seem much doubt that he used Black Israel to recruit, or develop, potential spies. I'd guess from what Hefler told me about Land's background, that the race riot made him ripe for subversion, and then Black Israel sucked him in. Black Israel also made its contribution to psychological warfare, by stirring up interracial strife in an arsenal city like Detroit. The web has more than one strand, and it looks to me as if Anderson sat in the center of it."

"You think he's the head of the organization, then?"

"I can't say. We've got so pitifully little to go on so far. I admit he didn't strike me as particularly big, or particularly dangerous. But I gave up spot judgments long ago."

Eric returned with a guarantee that Doss would be available when he was wanted. Gordon began to ask him questions about Land's disappearance. I told them I had a date, and went ashore. The Officer of the Deck gave me a jeep to the main gate of the Repair Base, and I took a taxi from there. It was barely nine, and I had plenty of time to get to the hotel by ten.

On the way I decided to stop at the Santa Fe station for my bag. Eric had lent me the use of his razor, but I needed a change of linen. The taxi let me out at the side entrance of the station, and I asked the driver to wait.

The baggage room was crowded with sailors retrieving their sea-bags and foot-lockers, a few drunks there for the company, a few civilians in clothes that looked a little frivolous and a little pathetic among all the lean blues. The clothes of a woman at the counter caught my eye particularly. She was wearing a tall felt hat trimmed with long iridescent feathers, gold pendant earrings, and two silver foxes which curled amorously around her neck but stared with cold button eyes.

The counter was lined three deep but I moved towards it. A sailor said without looking at me: "Hey, quit your shoving!"—then turned and added, "Sir."

The woman with the foxes looked around and caught my eye. She gave no sign of recognition, and quickly looked away again. But not before I had recognized the rouged and raddled face of Miss Green.

I said, "Miss Green," but she didn't look around. I pushed slowly towards her but before I reached her she left the counter. The sailors made way for her and she was at the door before I could work my way out of the crowd.

I caught her on the sidewalk and took her arm. "Miss Green, I'd like to talk to you."

"Let me go, I don't know you." I looked closely into her face in the light of a streetlamp, and saw that her eyes were empty and hot. But it was not the evil look in her eyes which went through my brain like a knife and quivered there. It was the odor of ether on her breath.

13

SHE tore her arm from my grasp and ran laboriously on high heels to a long black sedan which was parked ahead of my taxi. A man in the front seat who seemed to be wearing a chauffeur's cap opened the door for her. She climbed in, the door slammed behind her, the black car jumped forward with the long rising whoop of a powerful engine, and Miss Green was out of my life again. But not forever.

I jumped into my taxi and told the driver to follow that car.

"I will if I can," he said as he shifted gears. "That's a Cadillac."

When we turned the corner the black car was out of sight. We took a chance on the next corner and saw it a block ahead at Broadway, held up by a red light.

"Slow up," I said to the driver. "I don't want them to know they're being followed."

"Say, what is this? Are you in Naval Intelligence?"

"I'm working on a case with the FBI."

"No kiddin'? Wait till I tell the boys."

"There won't be anything to tell them if you lose sight of that car."

"Brother, I'll run this crate down to an oil spot before I lose 'em."

Before we reached the intersection the light changed. As the black car leapt away I caught a glimpse of an old evil face at the rear window. I took off my hat and held it in my hands and crouched low in my seat. There was heavy traffic in downtown San Diego that night, and maneuverability was more important than speed. My driver took his cab through impossible openings which closed a foot from the rear fenders. He aimed nonchalantly into traffic snarls which opened up like the Red Sea just before we piled up in them. We curved and skidded across the southern half of San Diego, past the all-night movies, the seedy restaurants and mushroom hamburger stands, the penny arcades, the liquor stores and warehouses, the storefront churches and four-bit flophouses, past the fish factories and the junk yards. Out of San Diego and through National City we kept the black car in sight.

On the other side of National City it accelerated. Its taillight went away from us like a small red comet and was swallowed up by the night. Simultaneously I became aware that I was on the last lap of my long ride from Detroit to Tia Juana.

The driver drove hard for a few minutes, his motor vibrating like a donkey engine. I bounced around in the back seat as the cab climbed and descended the looping coastal hills. At Palm City he slowed down and said over his shoulder:

"I tore the guts out of this baby, but she's out of her class trying to catch a Cadillac. God damn it."

"This is the road to Tia Juana, isn't it?"

"Yeah, it looks like they're going to Tia Juana."

"Will you take me there?"

"You're the boss. I'll have to charge you special fare."

"This is what I've been saving my money for."

He accelerated to a steady fifty and drove for another ten minutes in silence. We topped a rise and saw the lights of Tia Juana below us. A few minutes later we stopped at the border.

"Did a black Cadillac sedan go through here a few minutes ago?" the cab-driver asked the border guard who looked at my I.D. card. Under the road lights I got my first good look at the driver's face: fat and forty, pug-nosed, with black Irish eyes. According to the license which was pinned up in front of me, his name was Halloran.

"Yeah. The big time. Uniformed chauffeur and all."

"You don't know who she was?"

173

"Nope. She's been through here before but I don't know her. Why? They cut in on you?"

"No. I just thought I seen her before."

"Some pan," the guard said as Halloran pushed in the clutch. "She looked like she just crawled out of the woodwork and was just about ready to crawl back in."

At the first corner in Tia Juana a barefoot boy with a flapping shirttail waved a pasteboard box and cried: "Gum! Chiclets!"

"Wait a minute," I said to Halloran.

"You come down here to buy gum?" he said cynically. But he stopped the car. The hungry-eyed Mexican boy boarded the car like a buccaneer. "Chiclets—two for a nickel!" he cried.

I held a fifty-cent piece in the light between the thumb and forefinger of my right hand. "Did you see a big black Cadillac sedan go past here a little while ago?"

"Yes, señor."

"Where did it go?"

He pointed to the right, up the hill to the center of the town.

"You're absolutely sure?"

"Yes, señor. That way."

"Do you know who was in it?"

"No, señor. American lady."

His eyes were on the coin with an intent and ageless gaze. His thin sallow face could have been anywhere between ten and sixteen. I dropped the coin in his box and he jumped from the running-board and ran away in the dust, his shoulderblades flapping through his shirt like vestigial wings.

We went up the little hill in the direction he had pointed, past weather-warped clapboard dwellings, tamale stands, the one-story establishments of cheapjack lawyers whose signs advertised quick and easy divorces. We stopped at a gas station at the top of the street, and I asked the Mexican attendant if he had seen my friend in the black Cadillac.

"Señora Toulouse?" he said, and widened his mouth with a leer which separated the hairs of his thin black

174

moustache. "I think she has gone home. She is your friend?"

"I met her on the train. She asked me to come and see her in Tia Juana. But I don't know where she lives."

"You don't know where she lives? Then you do not know Tia Juana." He leered once more, as if there were curiously amusing secrets unknown to those who did not know Tia Juana.

"That's right, I don't."

He turned to Halloran: "You know where the girls are?"

"Yeah."

"Señora Toulouse has the biggest house in the street. You will see it. It is built of stone."

I gave him a dollar, which he folded and tucked into his waistband. He stood back and leered us amiably out of sight.

"What the hell is this, anyway?" Halloran said.

We had turned into a noisy street which slanted down between brilliantly lighted houses into final darkness. There was a steady male traffic on the footpaths, and on the lighted porches girls like assorted fruit on display. Between the two, the men in the street and the waiting girls in the houses, there was a low tension which exploded continuously in wisecracks, obscene repartee, and invitations.

We stopped at the first corner and a lean dark youth in a white open-necked shirt appeared from nowhere. He said: "You want something very, very nice?"

"I'm looking for Señora Toulouse."

"Señora Toulouse phooey," he said ardently. "They are old stuff and also they supercharge. You come with me. I show you something." He opened the back door of the cab, leaned forward with his hand on my knee, and whispered: *"Virgin!"*

I gave him a dollar and said: "Where is Señora Toulouse?"

"Si, señor," he said courteously. "It is there. The big house in the middle of the block." He leaned forward again: "Will you tell her Raoul sent you? Raoul?"

175

I almost closed the door on his narrow, hopeful face. We moved down the road and parked across the street from the big house. It was an imposing mansion of grey stone, not indigenous to the country but squarebuilt like old Ohio farmhouses. It had three stories, all of which were lit, but blinds were drawn over every window. The front door was shut and there were no girls on the porch, but there was the sound of music from inside.

"I'm going in," I said. "If I don't come out in half an hour go to the police."

"No use going to the police. You know what this is, don't you? These cathouses are protected by the local cops, that's why they're here."

"Go to the police at the border. Then drive back to Diego and go to Mary Thompson at the Grant, got that? Tell her—wait a minute, I'll write a note."

I tore a page out of my address-book, wrote a note to Mary telling her to get in touch with Gordon, addressed it and gave it to Halloran. "This is if I don't come out in half-an-hour. It's ten now."

I paid him his fare and some extra, and got out of the cab. I felt awkward and light as I walked up the steps with Halloran's black eyes on my back, and knocked on the heavy carved door.

A rectangle of face containing two small eyes appeared at a Judas hole. The eyes gave me a once-over, the Judas hole snapped shut, and the door opened.

"What can we do for you?" the doorman said. He was pig-eyed and pig-bodied, shaped like a Japanese wrestler and as wide as the door. His accent was Minnesota Norska. I wondered automatically how deep my fist would sink in the swelling dough of his belly.

I said I would like to see Madame Toulouse.

"She ain't home. Now if you want a good time we can do business with you. If you don't want a good time we can't do business with you."

I said I was crazy for a good time, and he ushered me through swinging glass curtains into a high wide room where the music was. It came from a piano and a guitar at the far end of the room, played by two cadaverous young men with shining black hair. The walls of the room, which must have taken up nearly the whole first floor, were lined with tables at which men sat drinking, some with girls on their knees.

The center of the room was a dance-floor where the rest of the girls danced with each other or with whatever male partners they could get. The girls wore no clothes, except that some had colored plumes projecting from their powdered buttocks. One had a red feather. One had a blue feather. One had a green feather. These plumes wagged like languid tails as the girls jigged through the bored routine of dancing. The girls with male partners seemed less bored, if you did not look at their faces.

"You can see, we got variety," the doorman said. "White, black, brown. Blonde, brunette, redhead, fat, skinny, Mexican, Chinese. Anything you want, we got it. You pay the waiter for your drinks and you pay the girl when you take her upstairs. You take your time and you take your pick. That's the way it works out best."

I sat down at an iron-legged table by the door and he retired ponderously through the glass curtains. They clicked behind him like unheeded admonitory tongues. The waiter, whose clean white coat insisted that the joint had class, came to my table and I ordered Mexican beer. The unattached girls began to converge on me like hens at feeding-time. Like figures in the dream of a naïve and hopeful hermit, they formed a half-circle about me, leaning forward and kissing the air with writhing carmine mouths and sliding pink tongues. In several languages they said the same thing, and their voices blended in an obscene cooing and twittering. Their breasts swung forward and the rouged tips looked at me like sullen eyes.

I got out of my chair and they gathered about me, making their eyes swoon and sparkle, their blackened lashes flutter in mechanical glee. I moved to the door, wondering if the body of a woman would ever seem good to me again, and escaped through the glass curtains. The doorman was sitting in an armchair across the hall. He looked up at me in surprise. Halfway down the wide staircase Miss Green turned and started back up.

177

I went after her. The doorman took me by the waist from behind, and before I could turn had locked my arms in a full Nelson which pressed painfully on the back of my neck. I struggled in his grip and got nowhere. My coat ripped at the shoulder seams.

"Let him have it, Jake," Miss Green said from the top of the stairs.

He let go with his right hand but held me with his left. A small heavy object came down dully on the back of my head. My body reverted to protoplasm and my mind to darkness.

When consciousness returned it came slowly and laboriously like an ambitious chunk of sentient organic matter climbing the stages of evolution from the original warm mud. I pulled myself out of the sucking black slime, the whirling waters that covered the earth, and lay eventually in a dry light place with my cheek on grass. But I found when I opened my eyes that it wasn't grass. It was a pastel-green rug lit not by the sun but by electric light. I heard voices and tried to sit up. I couldn't sit up because my wrists and ankles were tied together behind me.

I raised my head from the rug and the blood beat at the base of my skull like an iron fist. What I could see of the room was bare, pleasant and strange. The only furniture I could see was the end of a chaise longue upholstered in bright rich silk, and a fragile table holding a slender vase of flowers. On the wall there was a wash-drawing of birds, with a conical white mountain in the background, done in faint and delicate colors. The rest of the wall was naked, except for a long curved sword in a gold-embossed scabbard which hung horizontally above my head.

A woman's voice was saying in a sibilant birdlike chirp: "It would not be wise to kill him here. I forbid it."

"I agree, Baroness," Anderson said. "I absolutely agree. We'll take him out to the ranch."

I craned my neck and saw at the foot of the chaise longue a small black slipper which flipped up and down impatiently on the tip of a silk-clad toe. "It will be necessary to transfer him with great discretion," the voice chirped. "Attention *must not* be attracted to this house. It

178

is safe now because we have been very careful. We will continue to be careful."

"We'll put him to sleep again before we take him down," Miss Green said. "I'll go down and get Jake's blackjack."

"No you won't," Anderson said. "I don't want him to be sapped again. I don't want his skull damaged. I've got a use for his skull."

"You are quite clever, Lorenz," the bird-voice said.

"I try to find a use for everything," Anderson said complacently. "I'm glad Drake dropped in, as a matter of fact. Hector is too big."

"I am sorry you came here," the bird-voice said. "At all costs we must avoid the serious attention of the police."

"It's my business that'll be ruined if they come here," Miss Green said. "But I had to bring him. Jensen wasn't safe in San Diego."

"You can say that again," Anderson said. "I even spotted a plain clothes man at the border, but they don't pay much attention to chauffeurs."

"It is not only your business that will be ruined if the police come seriously, Miss Toulouse," the bird-voice said. "More intimate values than the financial are at stake."

"Don't I know it," Miss Green said. "Let's get him out of here. And I still say sap him."

"We won't sap him again," Anderson said firmly. "It might leave a dent on his skull. We'll put him to sleep with ether."

"Not my ether you won't. I have a hard time getting that stuff. I damn near went nuts those last two days on the train."

"Get your ether," Anderson said.

"Like hell I will. You can gag him, can't you?"

"Get your ether," Anderson said. There was the sound of a blow on flesh and a low female sigh. A woman's footsteps crossed the rug behind me and left the room.

"I don't like to see you mistreat women," the bird-voice said. "It is destructive of harmony. Perhaps one day you

179

will be punished, Lorenz." The speech left flat tinny echoes of menace in the room.

I thought it was time I entered the conversation. "You're damn right he will."

"Why, Ensign, it's nice to have you with us again," Anderson said. "Say, turn around and let me look at you. There's nothing I like better than the face of an old friend."

He took me by the hair and pulled me around so that I faced into the room.

"Don't forget," the bird-voice said. "You do not wish to damage his skull."

"Hell, the hair and scalp don't matter." By way of illustration he took hold of my hair again, lifted my head and shoulder a foot or so from the floor, and let me drop. "It's just the skull I'm worried about."

The woman on the chaise longue whose voice was like a flat chirp had a tiny ivory-tinted face above which balanced carefully coiffed masses of dull black hair held in place by a tortoiseshell comb. There was something dainty and old-world about her, an air which was enhanced by her dress. This was a flowing robe of blue silk, full in the sleeve and skirt, gathered at the waist under a broad silk waistband. The ivory throat on which her head was poised was small and delicate. My attention was occupied by that pure throat. I was intensely interested in whether the Samurai sword on the wall could sever it in one stroke.

I said: "Before long you'll be out of a job, Baroness. We'll tell you ahead of time where our ships are going to strike, and you won't be able to do anything about it. Shall I tell you more?"

The small woman on the chaise longue did not smile. From where I lay I could not tell whether she was a young girl or an old woman. "Be careful not to injure his bones, Lorenz," she said. "His other tissues are more or less beside the point."

Anderson kicked me carefully below the ribs and below the pelvis. For a minute nothing was important to me but the fingers of pain which searched my body. Then I said, very carefully so as not to shout: "You will not be able to

180

do anything about it because there will be no Japanese warships left. There will be no Japanese airforce left. Perhaps there will be no Japanese cities left. The Japanese islands will be a sad place."

"Are you tired, Lorenz?" the little woman said. He kicked me carefully in the lower part of the abdomen.

I said: "How did you ever get into the big time, Jensen? I thought you were a small-time crook. You still have all the mannerisms of a pimp."

He kicked me again, but without enthusiasm. I decided that I had contributed my share to the conversation, and fell silent. My stomach muscles were moving like injured worms.

Miss Green came into the room with a colorless glass bottle in her hand. There was a blue mark on her cheek under the red mark of the rouge, but she looked warm and excited. The hand which held the bottle trembled and the junk jewelry on her arm clinked merrily. Her step was quick and elastic.

"My God," Anderson said. "She's been at the ether again."

"I just thought if you throw away this bottle like you did the last one," said Miss Green. She executed several steps of an original *pas seul*. "Well, I just thought."

"Give me that bottle," Anderson said.

"Here it is, you fat stoat." She tossed it to him. He caught it, took a single threatening step towards her, met the impassive gaze of the Baroness, and turned to me.

He poured some of the ether on a handkerchief and applied it to my face. It scalded my mouth like fire or ice. I moved my head quickly and bit his wrist. He tore it from my teeth but I tasted blood. Then he held my head by the ears while the Baroness held the cloth to my face. I retired again into a universe of turning wheels.

When I came to I was lying on the floor in the back of a car which was moving quickly over an uneven road. At least that was the hypothesis which fitted the facts that dirty fabric vibrated steadily under my face and bounced intermittently against my skull with explosive pain. I could hear the hum of the powerful motor. I could see no lights.

I tried to flex my arms and felt the strain on my legs. My wrists and ankles were still tied together behind me. I began to rotate my right wrist in a quarter-circle within the loop of rope which held it. The rope was tight and rough and wore away the skin. I continued to rotate my wrist, working the rope down past the base of my thumb. I could feel warm blood on my hand. Perhaps it helped to lubricate the rope, which slipped gradually down towards my knuckles, wearing away the skin as it went. My hand felt as if it had been thrust in boiling water. I continued to work it back and forth within the loop. The rope slid over the thickest part of my thumb, and I jerked my hand free.

With my right hand I went to work on the knots which held my other hand and my feet. The blood made the knots slippery and hard to open. I hoped that I was not losing a great deal of blood. I wanted to have enough blood left to kill Anderson.

The knots had not been tied by a man who knew anything about knots. Once I got them started they loosened easily. My left hand came free without losing the skin. That was encouraging, because I needed one good hand. Inch by inch, so as to make no noise, I turned over on my back. I reached to my bent legs and removed the rope from my ankles. My hand simmered, my head rattled, and my stomach screamed. But I had accomplished a great deal.

Supporting myself on my hands because my stomach would not bear the weight, I rose to a sitting position. From there I could see over the back of the front seat the upper half of a man's head wearing a chauffeur's cap. I knew that the head silhouetted against the reflection from the headlights must be Anderson's because I hated it so much. I crouched forward and moved my arms, flexing and stretching them. When I was quite sure that they were able to do what I wanted them to, I flung my left arm over the back of the front seat and embraced Anderson's neck.

My stranglehold went on so fast and hard that his exclamation of surprise died in a gasp. But he had enough presence of mind to jam on the brakes. The car slewed

182

sideways on gravel which machine-gunned the chassis and fenders, and came to rest. Without deliberately looking I saw that the road passed among mountains along the edge of an arroyo, and that there was a moon.

I had Anderson's throat in the angle of my left elbow and began to apply leverage with my right hand. But he had managed to get a gun in his hand, which he used to hammer my arms and my fingers. I let go with my left hand to grapple for the gun, but my injured right hand was not strong enough to hold him.

He twisted out of my grip and struck me with the muzzle of the gun on the side of the jaw. I fell over into the back seat and before I could reach him again he was out of the car.

He opened the back door and showed me the snout of his automatic. "You drive the rest of the way," he said.

A .45 automatic at three feet was unanswerable. I climbed in behind the wheel and he got in beside me.

"If you go over fifteen I'll shoot you in the base of the spine," he said. "And stay in the center of the road. There won't be any other traffic."

The black sedan crawled up the moonlit road, purring like a stroked cat. Anderson's gun was thrust hard into the base of my spine. We came to a single-track dirt road which looped off to the right and ascended out of sight among the hills. The entrance to it was barred by a wire gate on a wooden frame.

"We'll get out and open the gate," Anderson said. "If my gun loses contact with the small of your back, I'll shoot. It will pay you to walk carefully."

I walked carefully to the gate, opened it, and walked carefully back to the car. The high slopes of the mountains were very beautiful in the moonlight, as beautiful as the white mountain in the drawing of the pale birds. I drove the car through the gate, and then we closed it behind us. The black sedan crawled up the narrow road among the hills. In a high valley flanked by mountains we came over the brow of a hill to a long low ranchhouse. It had a dim yellow light in the window.

Anderson told me to stop the car and I stopped it. He

told me to get out and I got out. He told me to walk towards the verandah and I walked towards the verandah. Hector Land was standing in the doorway waiting for us when we climbed the steps.

"This is the man that killed Bessie," Anderson said. "I want you to choke him to death, but be careful not to break any bones in his neck."

Hector Land's right fist struck me in the face very quickly, twice before I fell.

"You'd kill Bessie," Hector Land said as he stood over me. "You and the white people like you, you'd throw her out of a job and drive her to whoring and foul her bed and then kill her. You'd kill us off in Detroit, you'd drive us out of the factories, you'd drive us out of the streets. You'd call us the filth of the earth but you'd love our women. You'd love our women and you'd kill us. Why did you kill Bessie?"

He took me by the shoulder with his left hand and lifted me to my feet. There was a light foam on his lips. His right fist was cocked. I strained against his grip, but my shoulder was wedged in a vise.

"Don't hit him again, Hector. If you do I'll shoot you. I've got to have that body with no bones broken."

Land blinked at him stupidly and said in a changed dull voice: "I'm goin' to break all his bones, Mr. Anderson."

"No you're not. He's about my size. We'll dress his body in my clothes and put my ring on his finger. Then we'll burn down the ranchhouse with his body in it. The police will think it's me, and they'll stop looking for me. But if any of the bones are broken they'll be suspicous."

"Do you know who killed Bessie?" I said. "Anderson did. He killed Bessie because she was—"

"Shut up," Anderson said to me. His speech was clipped and low, but it had a raw edge of uncertainty. "One more word and I'll shoot." He took a backward step so that his face was in shadow. The outer rim of the circle of light from the doorway glinted dully on his automatic.

"I want him to say his piece," Hector Land said.

Anderson's gun moved slightly so that it included us both in its threat.

"You know a gun can't stop me," Hector said.

"Anderson killed Bessie because she was going to tell the police about Black Israel." My words poured out so fast I almost babbled. I didn't know when a bullet would put a period to them, but they were my only chance.

"It's a lie," Anderson said. "He killed Bessie, and he's trying to lie out of it. Stand back, Hector. I'm going to shoot."

Hector Land stayed where he was beside me. His face was blank and heavy, but his small black eyes shifted continually from Anderson to me and back to Anderson again.

"Why should I kill Bessie, Hector? Did I kill the others? Did I kill Sue Sholto?"

"I wasn't even in Detroit," Anderson said. His voice had risen a full octave as if fear had struck a tuning fork in his head. He still held the gun but it did not encourage him.

"This man tricked you into doing his dirty work for him," I said. "He pretended he wanted to help your people but when Bessie got dangerous to him he killed her. Are you going to let him go on using you, Land?"

"Put down your gun," Hector said softly to Anderson. "I want to talk to you."

His large body slanted towards Anderson in a slight movement which was as terrible as the slight movement of a stone statue.

Anderson said: "Stay where you are or I'll fire." The automatic shifted in his hand, and I saw his fingers tighten on the trigger.

All this time Land had been holding my shoulder, which ached in his grip. In the same moment he let go of me and moved swiftly towards Anderson in a crouching leap. The gun fired six times before it was knocked away. I jumped to the ground and searched for it in the dust, but couldn't find it. When I looked up Anderson was standing on the porch white and shaken. Land was stretched out at his feet. I rushed Anderson and hit him with my left because my right was injured.

He kicked at my groin but only grazed my thigh. I closed with him and hit him with my left. I felt his nose break under my fist. He turned to run and I caught him from behind by shoulder and crotch and threw him over the railing of the verandah. He fell heavily in the dust, lay still for a moment, and began to get up.

I went after him and waited over him till he got up. Then I hit him with my left. One of his teeth showed through his upper lip. He saw that I aimed to kill him and closed with me groping for a headlock. He caught my head in a thick arm and for a minute I teetered on his hip. I set all the strength I had left against his weight, which was greater than mine. Finally I slipped my head free. I put my knee in his back and dragged him backwards with my arm around his throat. He fell heavily with me on top of him.

When he got up I hit him again with my left. The lower half of his face was bright with blood. Now a flap came loose over his eye and hung down showing the white bone. I hit him again with my left and he went down moaning. I pulled him to his feet and hit him again with my left. He kicked at me but lost his balance and fell on his back. I helped him to his feet and hit him again. My fist caught him in the center of the throat and broke his larynx. I heard it snap. When he fell down I let him lie. I was very happy.

Hector Land came down off the verandah then. He walked slowly and the blood ran down one side of his face from a bullet track across his temple. But when he pushed me out of the way I staggered my own length and fell in the dust.

I lay there and watched him kick Anderson to death. Anderson's head became shapeless and muddy. There was nothing I could do and nothing I wanted to do. I was afraid of Hector Land and I wanted to see Anderson die. When I had seen him die I crawled around the corner of the house and sat in the shadow nursing my broken left hand.

14

AFTER a long time, during which my body was stiffened and chilled by the mountain air, I moved from my seat in the shadowed dust and looked cautiously around the corner of the house. Anderson lay where he had fallen, his face in the moonlight half-returned to indistinguishable earth. There was no trace of Hector Land except the destruction which I had begun and he had ended.

I left my hiding place and crawled in the dust below the verandah, clawing through it square foot by square foot, searching for the gun which Anderson had dropped. Not even the war had been able to convince me, but I was convinced now, that a gun was more precious than anything else. In a world of violence and terror a gun was the staff of life. My nerves were so shaken that I should not have been astonished if the mountains had spoken and threatened me, or if armed men had sprung up out of the ground. I sifted the dust for the gun as a prospector sifts gold-bearing sand, but I couldn't find it.

Then came the one remaining thing which had power to astonish me, and the mental horror was added to the physical horror. Far off among the mountains I heard the hum of an automobile engine like a drone of insects, which grew louder as the car climbed the road towards the valley. I could see the beam from its headlights, first like a small faint dawn working its way across the brow of the pass into the valley, then like a white flare of torches flung intermittently against the night. Before the car itself came into sight I went back to my lair and squatted down to watch. With my whole body weak and sore, and without a gun, I felt helpless and declassed, without rights or hopes in a world which struck unpredictably against anyone who did not have a weapon and the will to use it.

The car bounded casually over the last ridge as if it were on a familiar track. When it began to descend into the valley I saw that it was a light roadster with the top down. When it reached the bottom of the hill and stopped, I saw that a woman was driving. When she stepped out of the car I saw that it was Mary Thompson.

"Mary!" I shouted, and ran towards her on knees which were almost unhinged by relief and reaction from shock and fear. She walked quickly towards me. Her hair, ashy in the moonlight, was blown by the wind.

She said, "Sam! What's happened?"

I pointed to the body in the dust.

"Who is that?"

"It's Anderson. Lorenz Jensen."

Her mouth opened to scream and the tendons of her neck came out like fingers in bas-relief. She made no sound.

"Don't look," I said, and put out my hand to her shoulder to turn her away. But when she turned to me she had a small revolver in her hand. A wave of nausea swept through the middle of my body. It was almost more than I could bear to stand in a line of fire again, and to be invaded by the thoughts which sprang up full-fledged in my mind after long repression.

"How did you get here?" I said.

She put the hand which held the gun in the pocket of her coat. "I drove here to find you. I got your message from the taxi driver."

"How did you know where to come?"

"The police raided Miss Green's house. She told them where you were."

I was so grateful for her explanation that I almost wept. For a moment of terrible stillness, during which the mountains had seemed as unreal as cardboard and the moon a silver coin pasted to a low hollow ceiling. I had imagined that she was another enemy. The sky expanded again into infinite pure space and the mountains resumed their solidity.

Then the whole fabric collapsed, with a grinding like bone being crushed in my head. "Why didn't the police come?" I said.

While she was still hesitating on the point of speech, I struck at her. She stepped back out of my way and brought the gun out of its pocket. "Raise your hands. Walk ahead of me slowly into the house. Where's Hector Land?"

"He ran away," I said. "He killed Anderson and ran away."

"Land killed Anderson?"

"I told him Anderson murdered Bessie. But you killed her, didn't you?"

A sudden Gestalt which must have been preparing in my unconscious for a long time, held down by the will to believe in Mary Thompson, illuminated the past month in bitter colors. "That was why you had a headache and had to go back to the hotel. So that you could catch Bessie Land when she came home from the bar, and quiet her for good."

Her face groped for an attitude. It is terrible to see a human face empty of meaning. Her face was still beautiful, but I saw for the first time its essential lack of humanity. It was like a silver face cast on a screen, sustained in beauty by the desire of the onlooker who wishes away its unreality.

"Turn around and walk into the house as I told you. I want to talk to you, Sam."

I had thought that I knew her intimately, but for the first time I saw into her mind. She could pull the trigger easily because she could not imagine the consequences of killing, because to her human bodies were organic matter to be disposed of when it became inconvenient. She could betray her country because she had no country to betray. She could kill me easily because lovers were easy to find. I did as I was told.

The front door of the ranchhouse opened directly on the living room, a wide low room, heavily furnished with thick black furniture. There was a cavernous stone fireplace at one end, and before it a refectory table flanked by chairs with carved backs. The room was dimly lit by a kerosene lamp on one end of the table. Facing the fireplace, at the other end of the room, was a door which opened on darkness.

"Sit down there," she said, pointing the revolver towards a chair at the end of the table.

I sat down and she sat facing me, with her back to the dead fireplace. I began to plan to overturn the table on her.

"Keep your hands on the table," she said. "If you don't I'll have to shoot you."

That repeated threat was beginning to lose its terror for me, but I put my hands on the table. My left hand was swollen and blue and almost rigid. My right hand was crusted with blood where the rope had torn the flesh.

"You're having a bad time of it, aren't you?" she said.

I felt free from fear and extraordinarily light, but I was beginning to lose my interest in things. I saw everything clearly, without conscious emotion, with the wan objectivity of a cynicism which is reached at the bottom of despair.

I told her the truth: "This is the worst time now."

"Look, Sam. I gave Sue Sholto her chance but she wouldn't take it. She'd been suspicious of me for a long time, ever since she caught me marking the records one day in the record-library. When she heard about the leak of information that night at Honolulu House, she finally caught on. But I gave her a chance. I didn't want to kill her. I went to her in the women's room where she was lying down, I even offered her money to keep quiet. She said she wouldn't keep quiet. So I had to kill her. Hector Land almost caught me at it when he came up to the powder room to talk to me."

"You must be strong."

"Yes, I'm strong for a woman. But I don't want to kill you, Sam. I don't have to kill you if you'll keep quiet."

It struck me suddenly that Mary was a strange name for her to have. Mary was an innocent and feminine name, the name of virgins and mothers. Then I thought of Bloody Mary.

I said: "Did you ever hear of Bloody Mary?"

Her eyes were very pale, almost white. My mind was

working at top speed in a vacuum, quick to find allusions which would do me no good. I thought of Scott Fitzgerald's description of a woman who had "white crook's eyes."

"You don't seem to realize, Sam," she said in a flat tone. "I have to kill you now if you don't agree to keep quiet. This is your only chance."

I told myself that I would play for time. I was too tired to face death just then. "What's your offer?"

"Life. That's the main thing."

"Go on."

"You know that we can get along. Now that Jensen's dead we can marry." She saw no irony in her distaste for bigamy. "It's best that way, I've found."

"Was he your husband? No wonder you tried to steal Hatcher's letter."

"The last few years he was. It cuts down on the passport problem and a lot of other things."

"I told him he was a pimp," I said. "I didn't know how right I was. He let you bed with me so I wouldn't catch him sneaking off the train at Gallup. Didn't he?"

"He couldn't have stopped me," she said with a perverse pride. "I wanted you. I still do, if you don't make me kill you."

"What would we do together? Make love?"

"You needn't be cynical about it. I know how you feel about me. I could have you now."

"One of the dangers of getting out of touch with normal human values is this." I forgot that I was playing for time. "You make ghastly mistakes. Like murder. Like that one."

Her lips parted, her teeth showed, her eyelids crinkled, but the movements of her face did not convey the intent of a smile. All I could see there was the terrible blank naïveté of evil. "Maybe not right this minute. You look pretty tired."

I said: "What would my other duties be?"

She said: "The Baroness is dead. She committed suicide before the police got to her. Jensen is dead. Toulouse is in jail, but she doesn't count. She doesn't know the business, she doesn't even know where this ranch is. She's nothing but a graduate of a Paris bordello, a woman we paid for the use of her house. We could make a lot of money, Sam."

"How?"

"I've got the brains and the contacts. You're in the Navy, and you used to be a newspaper man. If you could get yourself transferred to Public Relations. There's a thing in New Mexico that Jensen has been working on. You may have heard of the Manhattan Project. We need an inside man, someone in the services, and we haven't been able to get one. You told me you wanted to make money, Sam. We could make more money than you've ever dreamed of."

"How much?"

"A hundred thousand dollars in six months." Her eyes glittered like glass, and I saw what her central emotion was. She loved money so passionately that she couldn't imagine how cold her numbers left me.

My emotions were coming to life again, forming a new configuration directed against her. I said in cold fury:

"I'd rather go into business with a hyena and make love to a corpse."

Her mouth fell open as if my sentiments surprised and offended her. "Don't you understand, Sam? I have to kill you if you won't cooperate. I have to kill you now. And I don't want to. Why do you think I took the job of watching you? Why do you think I didn't kill you in Detroit? I could have killed you there. I could have killed you in Honolulu. After his own attempt failed, Jensen wanted me to kill you on the train but I didn't want to. Even when you started figuring out our code I didn't want to. I thought perhaps we could get along."

I said nothing. I watched her face. I saw that like all true criminals she was abnormal. Part of her sensibility was missing and part of her mind was blank. She could not see herself as evil or depraved. Her ego stood between her and the rest of the world like a distorting lens.

My anger had died down into a kind of sick repulsion, but steady fear of the gun made my mind unnaturally active. I knew I had come to the end but I kept on talking. Talking had saved my life once. I did not see how it could save me again, but I went on talking, buying my life minute by minute with words. Perhaps the vigilance of the gun would relax, and I'd have a chance to move.

"How did you get into this kind of thing?" I said. There was a whine of insincerity in my voice which I couldn't repress.

"I hate the life." But she went on as if she had been waiting eagerly for such a question, as if perhaps she had not had a chance to explain herself for years: "But I've always been in it, and it buys me the things I want. I started lifting things in stores when I was eleven. There was a woman that pretended to be my mother when we went shopping. She was Jensen's mistress then."

"I thought your parents were in Cleveland."

"My mother died in Cleveland when I was a baby. My father took me to Chicago when I was seven, and died two years later. I've been on my own ever since. Jensen got rid of the other woman when I was fourteen, and then we started to work into the real money. I'd pick up men on the Chicago streets and take them to our apartment. Jensen would come in and pretend to be my father. I was underage. They paid. But the last one was a detective. Jensen went to the penitentiary and I went to reform school. When he got out he helped me to escape, but we were on the rocks and the police were after him for breaking parole. We went west and travelled steerage from Seattle to Manila. From there we went to Shanghai. We made some good contacts in Shanghai. Since then we've been in the money."

"Money is very important to you, isn't it?"

"It's very important to everybody, don't let them kid you. Maybe it's a little more important to me. For two years I slept in a box of excelsior behind a furnace in a cellar. I ate what people left on their plates in restaurants. Now I eat the best that money can buy."

"Human flesh is a rich diet," I said, "but it makes you deathly sick in the end."

I had found words that reached her. As if I had pressed

a button her face became convulsive. "I didn't want to kill them," she chanted in a high voice which rose to a scream. "I didn't want to kill Sue Sholto! I didn't want to kill Bessie Land! But she knew about Jensen and Black Israel, and she was getting ready to talk. I had to. It was hard for me. I did have a migraine that night."

A blob of saliva dripped over her lower lip onto her chin. I tried to imagine myself ever kissing that wild mouth. She wiped the moisture away with the back of her left hand. Her right hand held the gun pointed steadily at my heart.

I knew that she was ready to kill me, and I had to act now. I tensed my muscles to overturn the table.

Before I moved Hector Land spoke behind me, from the other end of the room. His voice boomed under the low ceiling: "It was you that killed Bessie."

Mary's eyes shifted from my face. I heard three heavy footsteps drag across the floor behind me. I watched her gun. The muscles moved in her slender wrist and it was deflected from my heart.

There was an explosion behind me, and her gun fell to the table. With one hand clenched on the edge of the table she held herself upright. The other hand was at her breast. A little blood leaked between her fingers and sparkled on them like rubies.

She said: "My breast is a nasty mess. You liked it for a little while, didn't you, Sam? You thought my breasts were beautiful."

She was about to say more, but she coughed, and her voice bubbled in her throat. Bright streams of blood spilled from the corners of her mouth, and for a moment I had the illusion that she was grinning a shining red grin which stretched from side to side of her face.

"It's just as well this way," she said thickly. "I didn't want to kill you."

Her eyes were black with pain and stared at me so intently that I didn't know she was dead till her body went loose. Her fair head, her mouth and breast, her fine weaving hips, her evil brain perched like an obscene bird

194

on the edge of madness, fell to the floor like a sack. A sack of food for worms.

I picked up her gun from the table and turned to face Hector Land. He squeezed the gun in his hand three times rapidly, so hard that the muscles in his forearm writhed like a black snake. No fire came out of the muzzle.

"A Colt .45 clip holds seven rounds, Hector. You've used the seventh shot."

He looked down at the gun in his hand as if unable to understand that a thing which had killed one could fail to kill another.

"You should be glad that you didn't kill me. You'll be better off if you'll come with me, back to San Diego. You've killed two enemies of the country, you turned against them of your own free will, and that may help you. If they put you in front of a firing squad it's a clean death, cleaner than the life you've led. A clean death is better than being hunted like a rat."

"Give me that gun. I got a use for that gun." He moved into the circle of lamplight, and I saw that there was death in his face. His skin was bluish and transparent, as if all his blood had run out. His eyes looked ready to die, lost and heavy with the sorrow and shame of his life.

"If you move again, I'll give it to you in the breastbone."

"A gun never stopped me yet."

He came across the rest of the room, swift and tremendous like a black waterspout. I pressed the trigger and saw a round spreading splash on his shoulder where the bullet struck. He paused and came on, so tall and wide that he seemed to blot out the walls and ceiling like a shadow cast from a low lamp.

I fired again, but he kicked the gun out of my hand and the bullet flew up between us into the ceiling. His eyes were unfocused and blinking as if the flash had seared his eyeballs, but his hands found me and closed on my neck. I hit him with my left and the pain gushed up to my elbow. A flap of scar tissue came loose over his eye. I hit him again and again, but his head rolled with the punches and

195

his fingers closed tighter on my breathing. I kneed him in the groin. He gasped but didn't let go.

The blood was pounding in my head and face, my lungs were sucking for air and not getting any, my eyes seemed to be expanding in their sockets. Somewhere near a dark waterfall was roaring, flooding the fields of my consciousness with night, rolling my bones down in its torrent with all the bones of the dead. My tongue forced open my clenched teeth, my knees became pitiable and remote like disasters in another country. I rushed down the dark waterfall.

But the iron collar was gone from my neck and it was only the floor I fell to. I drew a whistling breath, and another, and another. The waterfall ran into a subterranean channel and its echoes faded.

When I sat up Hector Land had found the gun and stood up with it in his hand. He said:

"You shouldn't try to fight me. I been in the ring."

He opened his mouth, set the muzzle of the revolver between his gleaming teeth, and fired. His brains spat on the wall behind him. They were no darker than a white man's. His body fell like a dark tower. The ruin was finished and the cycle was complete.

When the thunder of the final explosion ceased, the low room became very still. I had a feeling that I was in a cell hundreds of feet below the surface of the earth, weighed on by mountains. With something like panic scurrying in my nerves, I got to my feet and found the door.

There was a chilly dawn light in the sky. A withered grey mist hung on the forsaken mountains. The earth looked tired and unlovely, spent by its gross passions. I knew it would look that way to me for a long time wherever I was. I wanted to get to sea again.

ABOUT THE AUTHOR

ROSS MACDONALD was born near San Francisco in 1915. He was educated in Canadian schools, traveled widely in Europe, and acquired advanced degrees and a Phi Beta Kappa key at the University of Michigan. In 1938 he married a Canadian girl who is now well known as the novelist Margaret Millar. Mr. Macdonald (Kenneth Millar in private life) taught school and later college, and served as communications officer aboard an escort carrier in the Pacific. For over twenty years he has lived in Santa Barbara and written mystery novels about the fascinating and changing society of his native state. He is a past president of the Mystery Writers of America. In 1964 his novel *The Chill* was given a Silver Dagger award by the Crime Writers' Association of Great Britain. Mr. Macdonald's *The Far Side of the Dollar* was named the best crime novel of 1965 by the same organization. *The Moving Target* was made into the highly successful movie *Harper* (1966). *The Goodbye Look* (1969) was a national bestseller for more than three months, and *The Underground Man* (1971) even surpassed it in sales and critical acclaim.